A Woman Endures

Marilyn Hering

A WOMAN ENDURES

PROMINENT
BOOKS
EDGE

5830 E 2nd St, Ste 7000 #9983
Casper, WY 82609
USA

Other novels in the Paterson Series by Marilyn Hering:
A Woman Possessed
A Woman Beloved
and also, An Irish Girl

For Walter, always

Our memories are the only paradise from
which we can never be expelled.
                              -Jean Paul Richter
                              1763-1825

"Set me as a seal upon thy heart, As a seal upon
thine arm: For love is strong as death..."

Eleanor and Dr. Aaron Kirov sat trembling in Dr. Birnbaum's office. She looked at the seven or eight pregnant women sitting there as well, mostly dressed in garments with teddy bears or dolls on them, their bodies protruding as they carried their precious babies. She wore a large smock covered with rosebuds to help disguise the fact that she showed no signs of as much protrusion in her stomach area as she should for a woman seven-and-one-half months pregnant. Kirov had been urging her to see Dr. Birnbaum a few months now and so here she finally sat. She still had hope. She had read stories about women who delivered children not even realizing they were pregnant. Perhaps she carried her child in such a way.

"Eleanor Kirov," the obese nurse announced and she entered Dr. Birnbaum's office. She had known him quite a while for he had once been the attending physician where she worked at the Women's Alliance in the poorer sections of Paterson.

The exam room had an aura of sterility with white walls and stainless steel fixtures. It reminded her of how she was feeling.

"Please remove your smock and all clothes," the nurse advised.

Dr. Birnbaum soon entered, a short chubby man with a full gray moustache. He frowned.

"Well, well, well. Am I finally seeing you?" His voice had an odd gutteral sound. "It must be at least four months since you've been examined. I'm surprised at you, Eleanor. You, of all people, know the importance of examination at least monthly. Legs up now."

She placed her feet in the cold stirrups.

His face became lifeless as he observed her flat stomach.

"And you are seven-and-a-half months pregnant now. Am I right?

"Yes."

He applied his stethoscope in five or six different places to the tiny bump that was her stomach.

"Has the baby been moving at all?"

"No." Her eyes filled with tears. "Not at all." She felt as though she had ashes in her mouth as she spoke.

He again applied the stethoscope to her stomach and listened even more carefully and longer than he had done before.

"I'm sure you're aware that your stomach area should be at least five times its size if you are carrying a thriving baby."

He held her hand.

"Eleanor, I'm so sorry. But your baby doesn't seem to have a heartbeat."

Finally the words had been said, the words she had feared hearing for so long. She thought of Aaron and the devastation he would experience at the news, although he was a doctor and certainly must have expected to be told something he already knew and Eleanor feared hearing.

"It's impossible for me to --remove-- the baby now. I have at least eight other patients waiting, plus I have to get to St. Joseph's to fulfill my duties there. Come to the hospital six o'clock sharp tomorrow morning so that I can--remove-- the baby. Eleanor, I must assure you this does not mean you can't have more beautiful, healthy children. We know so little about these things, really. Hopefully, someday we will know more. I'll induce labor tomorrow under anesthesia. You will feel no pain. Your cervix has not begun to dilate and I'll insert some medicine into your vagina to start the process. And we'll give you a hormone to stimulate the uterus' role. I'm quite sure you'll be able to deliver vaginally then."

She whipped her hand away from him and began to wrench her hands.

"Why did this happen to me when so many babies are born healthy? I did everything right. I ate the proper foods, exercised. Tell me!" Her heart thumped so hard it almost hurt.

"If only I could answer that question."

The nurse helped her from the stirrups and table and put her clothes on.

She saw Aaron sitting in the waiting room. He approached her as she came to him and fell into his arms.

"The baby--is dead. But you knew that all along, didn't you?"

He hesitated, then said, "I suspected it. But I didn't know if you were ready to hear it from me. I thought hearing it from Dr. Birnbaum would be best."

The next morning at six o'clock they arrived at the office. Dr. Birnbaum arrived shortly after.

"It's better we remove the baby now. It's almost eight months. I hope you haven't developed an infection or blood clotting problems." He sighed. "You were so foolish to wait so long."

The nurse helped her undress and she placed her feet in the stirrups.

Dr. Birnbaum noted Eleanor's cervix had not begun to dilate in preparation for labor and inserted medicine in her vagina to start the process as well as a general anesthetic.

With much pushing and pressure on her part, he removed the baby and handed it to the nurse.

"I want to hold it."

Eleanor was adamant, her heart splintering.

Birnbaum frowned.

"It's not the usual procedure."

"Please..."

"Well, since you are a nurse yourself I think it would be all right, but just for a minute or so. It may help your future healing."

It was a girl, stiff, like light blue porcelain, covered with phlegm, wet and slimy, with a beautifully formed face. Eleanor touched its face and began to weep.

Then she noticed what Dr. Birnbaum would later explain. Most likely because of a nuchal cord accident, the umbilical cord was wrapped tightly around the baby's neck. Otherwise she would have become a perfectly formed live little girl.

Eleanor remained in grief in the hospital one day and night, then left with Aaron by her side, half aware.

"Could we go to the Great Falls, Aaron?"

"Of course."

He held her arm to steady her, although she now appeared quite all right, bodily at least. She could not go back to her nursing position at the Women's Alliance quite yet she knew. So she went to the one place that always gave her a feeling of comfort, peace and tranquility. Water gushed from the Great Falls full force for it had been a wet spring. They flowed in full splendor. She stood by the railing with Aaron and now and then could feel the tiny droplets upon her face. It was as though they had healing power. But could anything heal her now as the deep sense of emptiness and loss permeated her?

They sat down on a bench and she thought of the baby. The clothes they had bought, the crib, the room painted creamy yellow since they were not sure it would be a boy or girl. She decided then in that moment she would never put herself in this situation again. There would be no more children. But Aaron must never know.

She stayed home a few days and became restless. After a week she returned to the Women's Alliance. It was a busy place when she arrived. Nora was taking a child's temperature and six more people were standing and sitting in their tiny waiting room.

"Eleanor, I'm glad to see you," Nora said.

"I'm glad to be back."

Work was a great healer.

She called in the next patient, a child with a sweaty face. She took his temperature while his mother watched with a frightened look.

"I'm afraid his temperature is one hundred and three. Were there any other signs he wasn't well?"

"He was coughing and vomiting today."

"I feel we should keep him over night. We'll start him on some medication."

"I'll be back first thing in the morning."

Eleanor noticed the hand towels were depleted when she went to get a hand towel to wipe the child's face.

"I'm going downstairs to the storage supply room to get some hand towels."

Nora immediately dropped what she was doing and ran across the room to Eleanor.

"No! I'll get them."

"For heaven's sake, Nora, I'm not too weak to climb stairs and get a few hand towels. If I were, I'd have still stayed home."

"Please, Eleanor, let me go."

"Nonsense."

She opened the door to the basement and walked down three stairs. Directly below her she saw Aaron and Brigitte, the other nurse at the Alliance, in a passionate embrace, a look of ecstasy on both their faces. Eleanor's heart began to thump wildly. She felt so overwhelmed by what she was witnessing she missed her footing on the fourth step and came tumbling down to the ground, landing on her stomach.

"Eleanor! What in God's name--"

Aaron was immediately by her side. She tried to push him away. That was all she remembered before she fell into unconsciousness.

She lay in bed at St. Joseph's Hospital; and her father, Colin, sat in a chair by her side.

"Oh my darlin' girl. What you've been through. But you must stay strong."

And then another man entered, Dr. Brodsky, the psychiatrist she had been seeing for a time.

"Eleanor, I'm so sorry for all that's happened. Eleanor?" He could see that she was half dazed. "I'm sending you to Red Stone Asylum, but you'll be at Level 1. There's just so much a person can stand before she needs a rest from the agony that occurs sometimes in life. And I want you to think of it that way. You'll be in a lovely room surrounded by gardens galore, your passion, as I understand. I have left word you are to have no visitors, except your father. You need to heal. I'll stop by to see you each day if I possibly can in the late afternoon, after my sessions. I know you will improve."

She half heard what he was saying.

"The asylum," she murmured.

"Many men and women go there for a rest. The staff will be at your beckoning. You and I will sort things out. You can be sure of that. But only when you're well enough and can think clearly."

She relented, for she was intelligent enough to know when she desperately needed help.

Eleanor had been to Red Stone Asylum before with Colin, as a visitor. His aunt had been incarcerated there at Level 3, which was for the seriously and or dangerously mentally ill, as well as Aaron's wife, Anna, who burned to death in a fire, as did Eleanor's aunt.

She arrived, silent in her grief, with an ache in her heart too deep for any kind of comfort. Aaron had betrayed her; and, worse, she still loved him with a passion even beyond her comprehension, even after the ecstatic embrace she saw him in with Brigitte. She arrived, bereft of hope, a grievous feeling within her, exhausted by heartache after what had happened, first with the death of her beautiful baby girl, and then the incident with Aaron. She was grateful Dr. Brodsky had left orders Aaron not be allowed to see her for all he was going to do was apologize and he didn't know whatever got into him, and so forth. It was too late. She would file for divorce as soon as she got her mind together. She was not foolish enough to think she could make any decisions now.

She was pleasantly surprised when she saw her room. White chintz curtains embellished with roses adorned the windows, the room painted in a light shade of pink. An old fashioned white wicker bed and a chair and rocker decorated with the same fabric looked comforting. A lace tablecloth and table holding a hurricane lamp sat next to her bed. She looked out the window and could see nothing but a carpet of various flowers in bloom; red and yellow roses, marigolds, petunias, pink vinca, hosta, lilies, bee balm--so many others. She was anxious to go out into the garden and sit on a wicker lawn chair.

A knock at the door sounded. A tiny woman with a pinched face greeted her.

"I'm Mary McGovern, your assistant as needed. Please feel free to call upon me if you need anything, anything at all. We also have a recreation room with a lovely piano, a hobby room if you're inclined to paint or sculpt, and a game room where you can work on puzzles of any sort. The grounds, of course, all of them within this area, are at your disposal. We want your stay to be as helpful and meaningful as possible, one that will help you overcome, or accept and deal with what is troubling you."

She turned to leave, then turned again to Eleanor. "And by the way, I do not pry, unless, of course, you wish to speak to me about--things. Discussion will be only with Dr. Brodsky, your psychiatrist. He's a good man. We don't encourage group therapy but only self- healing. I'll leave you now so you can unpack and get acclimated to things. Remember, call me if you need any help. Any help at all. Just dial and ask for Mary any time of day or night. I have rooms here so I'm always available."

"Thank you."

Mary closed the door. Eleanor sat down on the white wicker chair with a fluffy pillow covered with chintz roses. She clenched her forehead.

How had she ever got to the point of being at Red Stone Asylum? Yet, it was not hard for her to imagine it as she thought back to her past life. Would she ever be able to go back to the Women's Alliance with Aaron's coming and going each day, feeling the passion within her each time she saw him? Over and over she told herself she wished she'd never see him again, but her heart told her something entirely dif-ferent. She loved him to distraction. She must face that truth. Obviously, he did not feel the same way if he could enter into such a frivolous relationship with Brigitte. And what of Brigitte, an excellent nurse? Why should she fire her and lose a good nurse as well as let the world know of her shame? Only one way of healing remained.

Time.

Time passed quickly at Red Stone Asylum. She enjoyed the gourmet meals, especially the lobster; but, above all, she loved to walk through the garden observing the flowers, some dying, some beginning to bloom, just like the circle of life.

To her surprise Dr. Brodsky had not come to visit her but called and said on second thought it would be best for her to try to enjoy her stay at Red Stone rather than have her experience his intrusive questions at this point. She smiled when he said that for his questions were intrusive, just as they should be, to help her get to the bottom of her misery.

But Colin, her father, visited every day after work. He would leave his position early to go see her. He was also now a part-time loom fixer, an important job, and he knew they did not want to lose him for his position at the mill was critical. The owners needed his expertise. When he left earlier than quitting time, they never complained.

"And how is my girl feelin' today?"

Colin smiled warmly at her. The two weeks would be over soon, and in his heart he was fearful of her return, though he tried not to show it.

"I feel so much better. I didn't realize how much I needed this rest. But how could anyone not feel better in such a place? Why, it's not what you'd think of when you say "asylum" at all."

His face darkened.

"But we know from your Aunt Coleen what it can be like. Eleanor, I have to tell you Aunt Colleen died and left a will, the letter said. They informed me two weeks ago but I didn't think you were ready to hear it."

Colin smiled. "And here's a good one to get you laughing. I am now a full-fledged tea plantation owner."

"What are you talking about?"

"Seems she and Charlie, her husband, had a small plantation in South Carolina. When he died, he left it to her. And she, in turn, left it to me in the will she wrote years ago when her mind was sound and she hadn't started to go downhill so bad. Anyway, the lawyer called me and it's all on the up and up. I have to go to his office in South Carolina and get things straightened out."

He snapped his suspenders.

"So you see I'm a full-fledged plantation owner. At least for a couple months 'til it gets sold. I thought I'd wait until you're doing real good and take you with me. See the country a bit before I put it up for sale."

Eleanor did not speak, but Colin knew a certain look she would get in her eyes when she was thinking deeply.

"Let's wait a bit before selling."

He scrutinized her face more carefully.

"I know that look in your eyes. Somethin's on your mind."

"I just need time to think. That's all."

"We wouldn't go until you were ready to travel."

"I wasn't thinking of that exactly."

"Well, what was it then?"

"We'll see. Let's just take things slow as possible for now."

"Surely."

She stared out the window. She seemed to be in another realm.

He left soon after, puzzled by the way she took the news. He assumed they would zip down there as soon as she was up to it and put the property up for sale, sell it, and make a fine profit which they could surely use to help with repairs around their home in Paterson.

But Eleanor's mind seemed to be going in a different direction. If he knew his daughter, he was sure she had something else, though he couldn't imagine what, on her mind.

Eleanor thought about the alternatives that lay before her. Soon she would be expected to return to nursing at the Women's Alliance. And what would that hold for her? The constant fear Aaron Kirov would walk through the door? The responsibilities of being in charge again, when, truthfully she still felt so shattered by the loss of the baby she had carried dead within her so long, plus Kirov's faithlessness, she did not feel ready to return, but she must not show it. She felt she must spend life with a mask across her face, disguising her real depression.

With her father's comment about his inheriting a tea plantation lay a possible answer. A new beginning. She would leave behind all the pain and suffering she had known and begin again. And why not? She certainly wasn't afraid of hard work; and, if it didn't work out, she could always return to Paterson. Perhaps by then she would feel strong enough to return to the Women's Alliance. Then, again, she and her father might love the Low Country and South Carolina as well as ownership of a plantation. Yes, she was ready for a change, for an adventure, to take her mind off the past.

Colin had grave doubts, but she finally convinced him. He conceded for her sake more than his own. He was giving up his job, his life at the mill, which he had known for years, to venture into a new environment he knew nothing about.

"If you don't mind me sayin' it, Eleanor, I don't think this plantation idea is a good one."

"And why not?"

"Why not? Now what do we know about runnin' a plantation?"

"We'll learn. And it would be a great adventure."

"I still don't buy it."

"Can't we at least go down there and see what's what?"

"Well, we have to do that anyway to sell it, if we do sell it."

Eleanor realized Colin was at least thinking about her idea.

She left explicit instructions with Nora as well as her address, which she made her promise she would give to no one. Nora would be head of the Women's Alliance until Eleanor returned, if she did. In her heart she planned never to return to Paterson. Kirov especially must never know where she was.

Aaron stood in the doorway, looking tired and thinner.

"I heard you're leaving the Women's Alliance and starting a tea plantation in South Carolina. This can't be true."

"We'll see. But you needn't worry about your living quarters. I'd like you to stay in the house, manage its upkeep if needed until I decide what I'm going to do. It may very well turn out that I don't like it down there and want to come back. But that does not include you in any way."

He approached her slowly.

"Eleanor, I beg you. Forgive me for such a foolish indiscretion. If you must know, and you can ask Nora as well, Brigitte had been flirting with me for weeks and I resisted her."

She stared him down, then seemed to pierce his eyes.

"Until now. And your excuses are meaningless. I had a lot of time to think at Red Stone. Whether I return I have no idea, not that it matters to you."

He grasped her by the arm.

"Of course it matters to me. I love you and always will. But I have to admit," his face became a bit flushed, "your refusal to have sex with me for fear it would hurt the baby, well, seven and a half months is a long time, perhaps especially more so for a man, I think. I really don't know the answer to that."

"Don't make excuses. Please. It's beneath you."

"But--"

"I have nothing more to say."

"At least let me know your address."

"Never."

He left the room, his head downcast, his shoulders hunched.

Colin was busy loading the car with the few belongings he was taking with him; and Eleanor packed a few dresses for herself, personal items, shoes and so forth. She expected the house would be already furnished. Starting anew, she was sure items like a kitchen set, bedroom set, and sofa in the parlor would be there. After all, Colleen and her husband had lived there many years.

She said her goodbyes to Nora, avoiding Brigitte.

"You must feel free to call me at this number or write me at this address if you have any problems at all. And promise me you will put it in a safe place. Tell no one the phone number or street address."

Nora nodded amidst her tears.

"I just hope I'm half the wonderful nurse you are, Miss Eleanor."

And then they were on their way.

After an overnight stop and much sharing of the driving, they entered South Carolina and the Low Country was not far off. According to their directions which had been sent by a Lukas McKendrick, they were quite close to the plantation. Along the way she could see women creating marvelous-looking designed baskets she was later to learn were braided from the sweet grass so prolific in the marshes of the Low Country. She stopped and could not resist buying a few. They were like works of art. She could barely understand the minimal English she was later to learn was the Gullah way of speaking. They had created their own language so their masters could not understand them, preserved for centuries when they were brought to South Carolina as slaves, mostly from Sierra Leone.

As they reached thirty or so miles from Charleston they passed hundreds of plants growing on both sides of the road in beautiful swaths that moved with the slight summer breeze that day. They had no idea what they were.

They stopped at a tiny store to get a soda and asked the proprietor, a bald man who had a habit of snapping his suspenders, what they were.

"Why, them's tea plants. Hundreds of acres of 'em. All owned by Lukas McKendrick, praise the Lord. If he didn't hire me, don't know what I'd do."

Eleanor's eyes widened. Why, her father actually owned a part of this vast area.

"Do you know the directions to the McKendrick land? There's a part that hasn't been cultivated in a long time."

"Oh, you must mean the McCullen place. It hasn't been touched for years. The only thing that comes up like clock-work is the tea plants, but they're all overgrown. Should have been trimmed for new growth years ago. But after McCullen died, well, his wife lost her mind with all the upkeep and losin' her husband. So it just sits there year after year. Mr. McKendrick, he's not too happy about it. But McCullen, he'd never sell. Neither would his wife. It's the one spot on the plantation McKendrick doesn't own. Must be a real burr up his ass."

The proprietor's face flushed.

"Beg pardon, ma'am."

"That's quite all right."

"Well, I sure enough can help you find the place you're lookin' for. Just keep drivin' like you are. Make a left at

McKendrick Drive. Then just go straight as far as you can. You can't miss it. It's real run down."

They finished their drink and were on the road again, made the turn as instructed. They drove through miles of thriving tea plants until they finally saw an extremely large patch of overgrown plants and a house that was as run down as the tenement ones Eleanor had lived in during her early life.

She sighed. What had she let herself in for?

"This is it, darlin'. Colin had taken out a piece of paper. I see the number on the door. One twenty four."

Eleanor's heart filled her chest, leaped to her throat even more as they walked up the run down path. She sensed Colin felt the same way. They had left their beautiful Victorian home with its wrap- around porch and the loveliest of furnishings for--this.

Their hopes were a bit rekindled when they entered. Aside from the cobwebs and dust, the house seemed in decent order on its inside, not having been ravaged by hurricanes. Each of two chairs plus a maple sofa was decked with a granny square, dusty afghan. Eleanor immediately thought of the boredom her Aunt Colleen must have experienced in such a remote area with the men constantly busy with the plantation work. Had that helped to lead to her mental collapse?

She inspected the kitchen, which she knew she eventually could place in fine working condition once she thoroughly cleaned. The same was true of the bathroom and the bedrooms. A sense of relief engulfed her. She could improve all this in time and have a cozy home. Thankfully, it was the outside that needed more repair, and she knew Colin could handle that with a nice paint job and some nails and other repairs.

She looked past their miserable tea plants, in tangles, but beyond that lay miles and miles of green, thriving ones. Alive. This is what she would try to do here, erase the stigmata of memory. She slept soundly that night and every other night. One word kept pounding in her brain.

Possibilities...

One morning a week or so later there was a knock on their door just as they had finished breakfast.

An extremely tall man who appeared in his late sixties at least, darkly sun tanned and wrinkled from the South Carolina sun and amber eyes, wearing a workers' uniform and a wide-brimmed hat, greeted her.

He removed his hat.

"Good mornin'. Hope I'm not interruptin'. Thought I'd come over and introduce myself." He held out his hand to Eleanor, then Colin.

"I'm Lukas McKendrick."

After the usual amenities he said his reasons for stopping by, which Eleanor knew in the first place.

"You needn't worry about this place, the house and plantation. I'm more than willing to take it off your hands and give you a good price for it too. You see, it's the only piece of the plantation I don't own. I offered your uncle, and then your aunt, a good price for it, but they just wouldn't sell."

At least he's honest, Eleanor thought.

"I'm afraid it's not for sale."

McKendrick scratched his head.

"Not for sale? You don't mean you two plan to run this plot of land and know not a thing about growin' tea, I'll bet."

"That's right."

"Tea's not that easy to grow. It can be temperamental. And then there's the hurricanes."

"I was told this is one of only three tea plantations in the states because of this area's perfect weather conditions for its growth. I have faith the plants will come back again. They're very resilient, I understand. Just need trimming desperately. Perhaps I could use your saw. I'd pay you for its use, of course; but Colin here is a crackerjack at repair work. So I'm confident we can make a go of it. And we'll surely need your advice."

McKendrick scratched his head again.

"I wasn't expecting this."

"Won't you think about helping us? With all your land, how can a tiny plantation rival yours? Please think about it."

"Well, I suppose I'll have to. You can't handle this, the two of you, yourselves."

"And of course we'll give you a percentage of our profits once we have everything thriving with your help."

"You really have caught me off guard."

"Will you think about it? That's all we ask."

He left soon after and knew even then he would help her and her father as much as he could. He hadn't seen such a beautiful woman--and he had been to many brothels to be sure. And he sensed she was intelligent as well. He led a very lonely life. Having this woman and her father around might be just what he needed. Why couldn't he be forty plus years younger? He wondered about her past. She must have been through hell to give up everything and come here to start anew. Perhaps someday she would tell him about it. Already he had her on his mind. This was not good. He had a plantation to run and he was an old man.

Nevertheless, the last thought on his mind before he went to sleep that night was Eleanor.

The next few weeks quickly became months, spent by Colin and Eleanor in straightening out their new home. Eleanor washed floors, dusted and waxed furniture, washed and dried bedspreads, slip covers, afghans and the like. Within a few months the house was waxed, shiny and clean.

McKendrick showed Colin how to work the thrashing machine and all the work necessary to run a tea plantation. When Colin wasn't doing that, he was working on the exterior of the house, the painting, the repair of roof and shutters, and weeding so that Eleanor could begin her precious garden. The house looked lovely on the outside when it was finished in creamy yellow with white shutters.

Eleanor could not help notice as they drove here and there in South Carolina that more and more flowers bloomed in this area and lived longer than they did in Paterson. She was anxious to plant a garden, flowers and nature being a part of her life's blood. She had mentioned to Lukas that once the house was perfect inside and out the first thing she would perform would be to create a garden. To her surprise and joy, Lukas had his men plant a garden for her. All sorts of flowers would bloom in it. A few she knew--a magnolia tree, of course--. But there were many she had to look up and learn about. She loved every minute of it.

As for Lukas, he thought he must be going through a second childhood to have a garden installed for her when so much other work needed to be done. But the men were no fools. They understood the great joy this woman brought to him and the members of the plantation in general. They were very happy for him since his life had been so very solitary.

One day, as chores fell into place, he took her for a ride on the thrashing machine and showed her how to use it. It was the first step in tea production he told her. Later that day and for a month or so they cut back the thirty to forty foot tea plants that grew on her property so that they could rejuvenate and begin to produce tea they were able to pick at arm's length.

"You've got some very healthy plants, Eleanor. I'm amazed at their resilience. If you would know the hurricanes they've survived, you'd understand better. Now that they're down to the right size, they should bud. That's where the tea plant is. I'll have some of my men help you with picking them."

She looked across the fields and saw the workers, mostly Gullahs, picking the precious buds.

"Next year yours should be ready for picking. It's that tiny bud- like tip that creates the tea. Someday I'll show you the whole tea making process. People don't realize all the work that goes into making a cup of tea."

She clapped her hands.

"Oh, Lukas, I would love that! I want to learn every-thing there is to know about growing tea."

He felt a surge of happiness rush through him. She was filled with such exuberance and excitement which was infec-tious. He hadn't felt this happy in years at seeing her joy. For though he was the richest man around, he had also been the loneliest.

A knock on her door sounded at eight in the morning the next day. Eleanor answered it and had already guessed it was Lukas.

"Good morning. Hope I didn't wake you."

"I'm usually up and around at six. I have trouble sleeping."

"I don't like to hear that."

"I'm used to it."

"I thought today since almost all the tea buds are picked you might enjoy seeing the process of how tea is created from them since, after all, now you're a tea grower yourself."

"I'd love it!"

They walked over a half mile or so to a gigantic building which, truth be told, she hadn't wondered about before.

"A tea plant needs a long summer and a great deal of moisture. Very few places in the United States have that com-bination. Some have the long, hot summer but not enough soaking moisture. And vice versa. Except in this area. There's only a few tea plantations in the whole United States. Did you know that? Most tea comes from India, China, Japan, and Sri Lanka. That's why we're so unique," he said with pride. He smiled. "Now yours is one."

"You can only create tea from the new growth on top of the tea bush. It's called a flush. It happens about every two or three weeks during the growing season. I'm sure you noticed the hundreds of men and women in the fields at different times picking tea. It's got to have 100 degrees temperature--that's why people hate this blasted heat when it comes, but it's great for the tea, and 100 per cent humidity. Now you can see why it's grown in so few places in the United States."

"I must admit; this weather is horrible."

He smiled, "You'll get used to it. Have to if you're goin' to be a plantation owner," he winked. "I don't know if you've ever tasted the other forms of tea. They all come from the same tea bush, but their flavor is different. That's because of the way the tea's processed. There's black tea, which I think you mostly know. That's fully fermented. Then there's oolong tea that's semi-fermented, my particular favorite, and green tea. That hasn't been fermented at all."

"I'd like to try the oolong tea sometime."

"Of course."

They moved across the floor and he pointed out the tea leaves she had seen workers pick in the field, now laid out on giant mesh wire belts.

"This here's the withering bed. They circulate warm air from below up through the leaves on the belt while they just sit there for about eighteen hours or so. That's when the tea leaf wilts and loses about fifteen per cent or so of its moisture. Are you following me all right?"

"Yes. It's fascinating."

He led her to another machine.

"This is a Rotor-Vane. Inside it's got a cylindrical chamber with real high speed rotating vanes. It's where the leaves are torn and break into millions of tiny pieces. Then once the leaf's crushed and torn, the broken leaves are placed on troughs about two to three inches deep."

"I had no idea all this goes into making a pot of tea."

"And we haven't finished yet. Unless you're tired."

"Heavens, no. I want to learn everything."

"Well, next they go very slowly along that moving belt, say, about fifty minutes. That's when the tea interacts with the juices from the broken leaf oxidizing and turning it from green to a brownish color by fermentation and that's what basically creates the black tea you've probably had. But you still have more steps to go. First you've got drying. Then they go to a moving belt that transfers them to a long oven. The heat in there's 250 degrees and for twenty minutes they stay in there and the fermentation ends. The moisture, as you can guess, completely leaves them and each minute piece shrivels up into a tight, tiny ball. All that wonderful flavor is now sealed in and it won't be released again until furiously-boiling water is poured over it."

"I'll never drink another cup of tea so casually again," she said, wide-eyed.

"Then near last it's sifted. It goes through screens of all different sizes to get rid of all the left over stock and fiber. Then we also pass the tea under rollers where static electricity removes even the tiniest impurities."

"What about the tea you called your favorite. Was it called oolong?"

"Yes. That's only semi-fermented. The fermentation process is fifteen minutes instead of fifty and it's a lot lighter than the black tea, more delicate and kind of nutty tasting."

"I can't wait to try it."

"You might even like green tea better. There's no fermentation process at all with that. After the tea leaves are picked, it's immediately steamed, then broken and quickly fired in the oven. It turns out a greenish color and it's pale and delicate in flavor. And now we have the last step when it goes to the lab for testing. There the tea testers check its color, body, and flavor. We employ four tea testers who do only that. Our tea must be perfect and we pride ourselves in it."

He turned then and saw Ed Colucci, a strange combination of the facial appearance of a cherub, a barrel stomach, and a body of iron, running towards him.

"Boss, I just heard it on the radio. A hurricane four is on its way and moving straight up the coast."

The explanation of tea preparation was immediately forgotten.

Lukas turned to Eleanor.

"You've never been through a hurricane before, I'm guessing. A number four hurricane is pretty bad. Five is the highest. The winds can go over one hundred fifty miles an hour and the storm surge eight feet. Get your father to go to the barn pronto. There's boards there he can use to nail down the windows, shutters, and doors of your house."

"Will it be that bad?"

"If it's a four and hits us it could be. Then again, it could go up the coast and miss us."

He turned to Colucci.

"Get going! Board up the house, the barn, the tea building. Thank God 98% of the tea crop's picked, and, hopefully, safe. Get the men to pick that last 2% and put it in the tea building for now. Then start boarding up. Pronto!"

Everyone scurried about around Eleanor.

"What can I do to help?"

"Help your father get those boards if you can and help him nail them up. I'll try to get over there to help you. As soon as you start to feel the slightest bit of rain or wind, you and your father come to my house. I've got a shelter built there."

"Surely it won't be that bad. We survived floods in Paterson."

"A flood is not a hurricane, believe me."

She trusted what he said and she was soon carrying nails and lumber to help board up their windows, doors, and shutters.

After about an hour or two an eerie silence fell over the land. The sun suddenly was covered with gray cumulus clouds that covered it completely. A strange dampness began to penetrate the air and a grayness covered the atmosphere around them. The silence lasted and Eleanor was beginning to think she was right about their being less danger than Lukas predicted.

Then it struck.

There was a great rumbling in the air so loud they could hardly hear each other speak. The workers, Lukas, Eleanor, Colin, and Ed were swept across the land. The roar of the storm quivered her frightened body.

"Get to the shelter," Lukas yelled.

After many setbacks from the harrowing winds, they made it. The tea pickers were already there. They had managed to pick the last remnants of tea and get it into the tea building.

They huddled in the shelter hearing the swishing and swooshing of the rain from the force of the hurricane's power. They could hear sounds of what was most likely the shutters, windows, and doors being torn apart as the hurricane pounded against the houses, probably battering all in sight.

The field, Lukas prayed, would not be uprooted and the hurricane would miss most of its destructive sweep.

They waited and waited. Minutes. Hours. Finally, the wind lessened a bit, but they still dared not venture out and risk being blown away. Finally, after a few hours passed quietude reigned.

Lukas was the first to open the hatch and venture out. He returned, his face white as paper.

They emerged and surveyed the damage. Shutters were either blown away across the yard or off their hinges, the winds stronger than the nails and boards that had held them down. The yard was a shambles of sticks, heavy rocks, and stones. Eleanor's garden was completely uprooted as well as Lukas' vast one. Shining rills of water ran in runnels. But one thing still lay intact, the tea building--sturdy and strong.

Eleanor saw tears in Lukas' eyes.

The plantation too had missed most of the hurricane's path, except for twenty or so acres nearest their home. And Eleanor and Colin's tea plants, though a few were battered and torn, ripped from the ground by their roots, had generally survived and eventually could be replanted.

She stood struggling for breath.

Then they saw the hurricane's eye must have shifted for a few hundred acres had been saved. Their blessed tea plants had remained largely intact.

Eleanor hugged Lukas hard. A shot of passion darted through him, one he had not felt so strong for a long time. He felt frightened by it. Her nearness went quivering through him, body and soul. Here he was, a man in his late sixties, embracing a girl at least one third of his age and feeling aroused. What the hell was the matter with him?

Eleanor, snuggling his shoulder, noticed nothing, then was well on her way to hugging her father and Ed Colucci, who had given them so much help in nailing down the windows and shutters.

She could feel Colin trembling, his eyes squinting in the shadow of his brows.

"We've lived through our first hurricane and came out basically all right. But, dad, there's so much damage-- the shutters, door, windows, so much else. And our porch. It's practically gone. Plus my wonderful garden." When she looked down at it, the ruined flowers, the wet and gushy soil, tears filled her eyes.

Lukas approached her.

"Don't you worry about your garden. My men will help you replant it first. You can be sure of that. I've lived through a hurricane number five years back and that was hell. So this is, of course, a setback; but we're used to it."

They looked at the massive destruction around them and thought of the mammoth task ahead of them: broken windows, shutters off windows, blown away doors, roofs lifted from their houses, trees blocking houses, mud everywhere.

Lukas gestured to Ed Colucci who came over.

"The radio said the storm surge was 10 feet and the winds 144 miles per hour."

"I want you to begin with Eleanor's garden. Want it replanted, reseeded. And put a magnolia tree in there somewhere. I want her to have one, see one in bloom."

Lukas walked away slowly, paper and pencil in hand, listing all that had to be done. Ed Colucci scratched his head. He surveyed all the destruction to be repaired and the first thing Lukas wanted done was to have Eleanor's garden replanted?

And then he knew...

After, the garden was replanted with a magnolia tree, dahlias, peonies, roses, black-eyed Susans, phlox, hosta, ornamental grasses, hydrangeas, bee balm, lilies, wisteria, a viburnum bush, and marigolds. They also planted a rambling rose which would eventually bloom near the side of Eleanor's porch, along with purple clematis and morning glories. Eleanor became more excited than ever for they had also enlarged the garden to accommodate vegetables, planting kale, zucchini, egg plant, cabbage, peas, carrots, celery and pumpkins.

She held Lukas' hand.

"Oh, Lukas, how wonderful! I never thought I'd have a garden here as lovely as this one."

"I'm glad I could oblige," he said, his heart pounding.

After the garden was refurbished, repairing damage from the hurricane began. Saws whirred and hammers banged all day long. This was done in conjunction with getting the tea to market which took precedence. Ed Colucci was in charge of its packaging, as he had been for years and transportation went smoothly, as usual.

As for Eleanor, she was so busy refurbishing her house she had little time for anything else, except think of Aaron Kirov. Time and again she told herself to file for a divorce and time and again she put it off because, though she hated herself for it, she was still passionately in love with him.

She relived the first day they met, his attempts to help her overcome her depression, gestures when he would touch her arm at the Women's Alliance and a surge of passion would spread through her, their trysts at the bed and breakfast in Hawthorne, their common tragedy of the death of their unborn child, which somehow bound them together, his suggestion she see Dr. Brodsky, who helped her so much. So many memories....

Right now she was baking an apple pie. She remembered Kirov told her that her desserts were even better than the ones he had had in Vienna. He seemed to enter into her mind every day, no matter what she was doing to avoid this.

And she knew why Colin wondered why she didn't file for divorce from a man she constantly told him was despicable and unfaithful. But Colin was wise enough to know they must settle their own affairs, though it hurt him to see a sadness in her eyes which he did not fully understand. Perhaps she missed Paterson. He left it at that.

Colin answered Lukas' knock on the door.

"Is Eleanor around?"

She greeted Lukas as he sat down in her kitchen.

"I've been thinking you've been working so hard on redoing the house and taking care of a hungry man for a year now."

"I don't mind that you eat with us. In fact, I enjoy it."

Although she often wondered why she was never invited to his house. In fact, no one ever visited Lukas, which she thought strange.

"Well, as a kind of thank you I thought I'd love to take you to Charleston. You know, it's a beautiful city, filled with history. And you haven't seen flowers until you see their streets and gardens. We can eat out at one of the best restaurants and have a great time of it."

"Oh, Lukas! Could we? You know, we saw little to nothing of it when we drove through it coming down. We were so excited to get to the plantation."

"How about next Monday? I've got to go to some meetings this week and want to make sure everything is supervised right before we take the day. It will be as much fun for me as you. I don't know when I've taken a day for myself just for plain enjoyment."

"Yes. That would be fine. I'd love it."

"Monday morning at 6 or so. With the traffic I want to get a good start, and have a full day."

He cleared his throat.

"Then, of course, some other time we can take Colin along too. He'd enjoy it I know."

But this time he wanted her all to himself....

Lukas took her on what turned out to be a grand tour of Charleston and she loved every minute of it.

They went to the Nathaniel Russell House that had been restored to the way it looked in the nineteenth century, one of the best examples of Federal style architecture in the States. She admired the ornate carved woodwork and moldings, the English silver and the famous "flying staircase" that was a free-standing spiral, seemingly unsupported, to the third floor. She also loved the English gardens adorned with all kinds of flowers, plus myriad bowers and lemon and orange trees which she had never seen before.

Then they went to the Row Houses on East Bay Street. They were famous for their row of colonial town houses. Lukas told her they were the largest intact cluster of Georgian row houses in the United States.

The area that interested her most was on Church Street, Cabbage Row, where in the 1920s he said poor residents of the tenement houses sold vegetables from their window sills, which gave the site its name. Lukas told her it was the inspiration for "Catfish Row" in DuBose Heyward's novel, PORGY, which she had read.

"Oh, Lukas, wouldn't it be wonderful if we could rent out a space near here and establish a clinic for the poor? I'm sure they're underserved."

"Well, it's certainly something to think about."

"And we could train people to work there and there'd be jobs for them as an outgrowth too. We'd need supplies and--"

"Now, now, don't get ahead of yourself. But, seriously, I do think it's a good idea. And you're right. The coloreds especially are terribly underserved."

"You're a good man, Lukas," she said, holding his arm.

The most memorable place for Eleanor, of course, was Magnolia Plantation on Ashley River Road, 50 acres of gardens that bloomed from the middle of March through April. There were about 250 varieties coloring the canal banks in brilliant pink, white, and purple as well as twisting wisteria vines filled with clusters of lavender flowers, sweet-smelling honeysuckle and pink and white dogwoods scattered throughout the property. Lukas said in summer the area was filled with summer magnolias, lilies and wildflowers and in fall and winter over nine hundred types of camellias were in flower.

"That's one fault of Paterson," she said. "Winter is so dark and dreary for the most part and you don't see a flower growing anywhere."

"All the more reason you should consider living here with your love of flowers," Lukas couldn't help saying. "By the way, are you as hungry as I am?"

"I'm famished."

"I'm going to treat you to a lovely place I know that serves Low Country cuisine. They're the marshy prairies that thrive in low lying South Carolina's coast, north and south of Charleston."

They enjoyed a wonderful lunch at Seafood Row of she crab soup, then shrimp, green fried tomatoes, ham, okra, oysters and crab ladled with creamy grits.

After that they shopped at old City Market in the afternoon, three blocks long with venders' sheds of all kinds, a historic market that stretched from Meeting Street to the river along Market Street.

Eleanor bought another lovely coiled basket made by a Gullah who signed the back of it for her.

"Coiled basketry came to South Carolina with the slaves from West Africa three hundred years ago. Before the Civil War the slaves winnowed rice and stored food in baskets made by coiling marsh grass with strips of palmetto leaves," Lukas explained. "They began producing and selling them, and now that's how most of them make a living. I love them. I have so many around my house; I collect them. They're very labor intensive. Take about twelve hours to three months to make, which adds to their value."

"I keep seeing signs with an arrow painted on them saying, "St. Helena-Gullah Country-basketry and souvenirs."

"The Gullahs live there and on other islands as well. They have their own language and culture. They're a community of coloreds who speak Gullah, a language with remnants from the slaves who worked the plantations on the mainland. They were kidnapped from their homeland and unable to communicate with whites or each other so they created their own unique language based on the different West African tongues. There are Gullahs living largely on St. Helena, Daufuskie Island, and Sapelo Island. Most whites don't mix with them."

"How despicable! I want you to take me to St. Helena sometime."

He smiled. "Your wish is my command."

On Monday of the next week Lukas took Eleanor in his motorboat to St. Helena Island. Ed Colucci stood by, along with Colin, who scratched his head thinking of all the work that needed doing on the tea plantation; but off he went with Eleanor, the happiest Colucci had ever seen him. Colin had hoped to go along but was not asked.

One of the Gullahs Lukas introduced as Len, with arms the size of small watermelons and smiled at them through yellowed teeth. He even towered above Lukas.

"You look busy," Lukas remarked.

"Dog got four feet but can't walk one road."

Eleanor looked confused.

"Basically, he said no matter how many things you'd like to do you can only do one at a time. Don't panic," he smiled. "The Gullah language isn't that hard to understand. Plus most speak some "regular English" too."

"And what is Lula up to these days?"

"Come in and see."

As they walked towards their house, in front of nearly every one was a man or woman making sweet grass baskets in various shapes and designs: rectangles, circles, squares--small, and large. Some were interspersed with darker strips that formed stripes; others were encircled with triangular designs. Eleanor eyed one of particular beauty with intricate pyramid designs of a darker grass woven around its sides, large enough to hold a bowl of fruit on her kitchen table. She gave the woman twenty-five dollars for it, as Lukas suggested, and she was more than satisfied.

Eleanor held it to her heart.

They approached Len's home and entered.

Eleanor was taken aback.

On each chair in the living room was a quilt, one more beautiful than the other. Not only were they quilts with squares, as the usual one is created, but Lula had embroidered red cardinals, gray sparrows, yellow goldfinches, and other birds on each square, along with roses, lilies of the valley, black-eyed Susans, and many other flowers and birds on the other ones. She sensed she was looking at works of art.

"Lula, this is my friend, Eleanor."

"How do you do, ma'am."

She was a tiny woman with small features, half the size of Len, in a long sleeved dress for such a hot day.

"Have you made these gorgeous quilts?"

Lula blushed. "Yes, ma'am."

"I'd like to buy one. One with the embroidered flowers. And I know many tourists would grab them up quickly when they come to visit St. Helena's. How many have you made?"

"Oh, I'd say about twenty-five."

"My goodness! And where are they?"

"They's stored upstairs in the attic in a trunk."

"You know you could easily sell them. You could get Len and his men to set up two poles and a rope across them and you can put them on display."

"My quilts? Does you mean it?"

"Of course I do. And all hand made?"

"Yes'm Got no sewing machine."

"Well, I'm going to buy you one. These are just too stunning to be packed away upstairs or in your attic where no one can see them."

"How much do you think a tourist would pay for them?" She could tell Len was curious.

"Well, I know I'd pay one hundred dollars for one. They're exquisite!"

"One hundred dollars! Oh, Lawd, I can't believe it."

"Next time I come back I'll bring a sewing machine for you and show you how to work it."

"I think it's a wonderful idea, Lula," Lukas said. "Let me know if I can help in any way."

"Would you like to stay for lunch?"

"We'd love to."

Lula served fried green tomatoes, salmon pie with a white cream gravy and grits, along with black tea.

Lukas and Eleanor said their goodbyes soon after, knowing they had left two excited people behind.

As they walked to their boat, she noticed in front of nearly every house was a man or woman still making the sweet grass baskets.

Eleanor was ecstatic.

"I'll always remember this glorious day every time I look at my baskets."

As they passed him by, another Gullah lifted his head and smelled the air. "Another hurricane, she comin'."

Eleanor was taken aback. "But nothing's been predicted."

"I'll go by Seth's predictions rather than any others. We've got to get back. Thankfully, the tea crop is safe and stored."

"Surely it can't be that bad."

"You've never lived through a number five hurricane, the worst. And I hope you never do."

When they got back from St. Helena's, Ed ran up to Lukas. "A bulletin just now came over the air. A hurricane four is coming."

"Lord, no. Lukas pushed back his hat. Seems like we just went through this. Get ready again. Tell the men pronto."

Within minutes men emerged from the house with boards and nails and began to board up the windows and doors of the buildings again.

"We're right in the path of it I'm sorry to say. But they said it could turn."

"All we can do, as usual, is our best to prepare. And help Eleanor and Colin by boarding up their house again. And their door as well."

"Yes, sir."

"Eleanor, go down to that shelter again with Colin and stay there."

"But there's hardly any sign of a storm."

"That's what makes them so malicious."

They carried some food supplies in case the storm lasted. Before she knew it, a stillness hovered in the air. Then houses shook and window panes the men hadn't had a chance to board up splintered to pieces. The rain came so rapidly and thickly she could not see the yard or outside areas. It blew the chairs from the porch down the way, knocked out her lighting. She and Colin huddled together and ran as best they could in the gusty rain across the land to the shelter Lukas had told them to go to. Then, miraculously, the hurricane turned and moved on, not like the first one that had lingered and caused so much damage.

Eleanor's teeth were chattering, Lucas held her in his arms and smoothed her hair.

"It's all right. The worst has passed us by to destroy some other place a million times worse than it did here. It looks like it's going to hit St. Helena's hard."

She finally began to calm down with the comfort of Lukas and her father.

A few days later Lukas insisted on going to St. Helena's to see how the Gullahs had fared and left his men in charge of repair work for his, Eleanor's and Colin's property. He took the motorboat and Eleanor insisted on going with him and bringing along her medical bag just in case.

St. Helena's had been ravaged. Trees had been uprooted and fallen on houses. Many homes had been so destroyed one could see their bedrooms, parlors, and kitchens from the outside. Mud covered their shoes as they walked to survey the damage and they stepped over trees that had been blown down.

Eleanor immediately went to Lula, who was shaken but seemed overall all right. She then went from home to home to give first aid to anyone who needed it. At first the Gullahs were skeptical of her but soon accepted her help in bandaging them, giving them medication for fevers which their own herbal remedies did not cure. She also set bones of some of the Gullahs who had been injured with broken arms.

"You angel from de heaven," one Gullah woman said to her.

Lukas gave Len a large packet of money.

"I want you to use this for repairs and just let me know if you need more. I've got so much money I hardly know what to do with it."

"You good man," Len said.

Eleanor heard that and the germ of an idea began to form in her mind. Why couldn't the Gullahs have a clinic and nurses and a doctor on call? But she had no time to think about it now with all the help the Gullahs needed.

When they had done what they could to help set things right and had surveyed their needs, they left, promising to come back soon.

As they were going back on the boat, Eleanor approached Lukas with her idea.

"Why not build a small clinic on St. Helena's where the Gullahs could go for help? After all, their potions and remedies aren't going to mend a broken leg or cure a cancer. They need a part-time doctor willing to visit. And a full time nurse. I can certainly go over to the island and show a few of the women how to set a broken arm or leg or the somewhat complex things they don't have remedies for. In time, perhaps they might even accept modern medicine."

"And who's going to finance it?"

"Well, it wouldn't be that expensive. I saw a run down building we could easily fix up with some paint, get some running water and heat in there, and supplies. And I can supply the money."

Lukas nearly dropped the steerage.

"I never did tell you I've been given some money by my first husband, Charles, and he's the type of man who wouldn't be happier if I used some of it for such a project."

"And, of course, I'd be willing to help all I can. I've got so much damned money I don't know what to do with it," he smiled.

"Well, you do now, Lukas," she smiled. "You do now."

"And we wouldn't take their own remedies from them--pellets of pine to alleviate coughs and sore throats, fermented filed cherry to cure diarrhea, hot broth from boiled willow root to reduce fevers, pulverized witch hazel leaves soaked in sea water to apply to aches and pains, so much of that sort of cure. It's the more serious things I'm thinking about."

"You're absolutely right."

"What about heart surgery, if needed? Relief from cancer pain? Things like that."

Lukas scratched his head. "Why didn't I think of this idea? And I'll explain it carefully, with your help, as long as it doesn't frighten them."

"And it must look similar to the other houses to make it seem more familiar."

"Of course. But first we've got to get their own houses in order after this other blasted hurricane."

"You have a special place in your heart for them, don't you?"

"Matter of fact, I do. I hate prejudice."

"You're a good man, Lukas McKendrick."

They made an appointment for the next week with Anderson and Graves, the best architects in Charleston. They specified the exact style of clinic they wanted.

"We want it to fit in with the look of the homes there already. But it must have strong windows to help combat the hurricanes, plus they can be opened to let the fresh air in. I believe that in itself can be a partial curative," Eleanor commented.

"Building could be started in the spring if our plans meet your specifications," Graves said.

Eleanor could not wait until spring, a few months away, and the Gullahs were as excited as she and Lukas were when they told them.

"Let's stop by and see Lula a few minutes. I know I told her I was going to bring a sewing machine next time I came, but I just didn't get to it with all that's been going on. I hope she understands."

Lula was caught off guard when they arrived and was bathing her arms which Eleanor and Lukas immediately noticed were covered with sores and scars, some healed and other parts of them scabbing.

She immediately rolled down her sleeves and closed the bottle of ointment she was using on them.

"Lula, roll up your sleeves," Eleanor insisted.

"Where in God's name did you get those scars and wounds on your arms?"

She would not answer.

"We're standing right here until you tell us."

She hesitated, then said, "Well, Len, when he drink, he gets mad at me a lot--and he hits me bad. But he don't mean it. He's a good man, but for the drinkin' Then it like somebody else in his skin."

"You mustn't put up with this any more." Eleanor began to check her medical kit.

At that Len appeared in the doorway.

"What you want?"

Eleanor grasped Len's arm.

"If you ever so much as lay a hand on Lula again, I'm going to report you to the police."

"How you know I hit her?"

"We know now why she wears those long-sleeved dresses, even in the heat of summer. We caught her off guard treating the bruises and wounds on her arms. You should be ashamed of yourself, Len. To hit a woman like that."

Lukas was as outraged as Eleanor.

"It's the drink. I ain't myself when I drink. Somethin' happens to me."

"Well, you better not do it from now on because the police will be called in. I can guarantee that."

Eleanor checked her nursing satchel and took out a more potent salve than the herbal remedy Lula was using.

"This will work better, Lula."

Len scratched his head.

"I swear to de Lawd I don't mean it. I love Lula."

"Then show it."

Eleanor snapped her satchel shut.

They walked to the door and she turned.

"I stopped by to tell you I will surely bring the sewing machine next time and show you how to use it. And by then I expect your wounds to be healed."

She glared at Len.

"And that there will be no other ones."

Spring finally arrived and building the clinic began. They made many treks by motorboat to St. Helena to supervise the building On one occasion Lukas had to go to a Tea Planters Association meeting. Although he was not happy to see her go alone, Colin could not accompany her either since he was sick in bed with a fever and a cold. She gave him boiled willow root to induce sweating and hoped for the best. Lukas said it was a Gullah remedy which had worked for him, and she was quite open to trying the Gullah healing practices before resorting to her own remedies. She felt it would also make the Gullahs more accepting of her, less suspicious, and she was right.

When she arrived at St. Helena and saw the great advancements they were making in building the clinic, her heart pounded with joy. The floor of the building was down and they were preparing to put in the frame. She stayed a few hours until dusk began coming on. She wished she knew the Gullah language so she could communicate better and vowed she would try to learn it.

The walk through the woods was her favorite time. The trees bent their limbs as if in prayer. Wildflowers popped up everywhere as well as some of the herbs she had learned to recognize: snakeweed, skunk cabbage, wormwood, horse-mint leaves, thistle blossoms, chokeberry, catnip leaf, wild cherry bark, sarsaparilla, dandelions, pokeweed, dogwood bark, wild lettuce--so many others she must learn. She was proud of herself she had been taught by Lula and knew many by sight now.

Suddenly, as if from nowhere, two men emerged from the woods. They blocked her way.

"Now, what's a beautiful white girl like you doin' walkin' through the woods where the Gullahs live, especially near dark," one said, a dirty, white-bearded fellow who had what looked like a red birthmark across his cheek, and tattooed arms the size of tree trunks, smiling at her through what was left of his yellow teeth.

She must try not to show fear.

"I'm--I'm going to my motorboat to go home."

He grabbed her by the arms.

"Give us a kiss, will ya?"

"Please, please! Let me go."

The other man with long, curly blonde hair in a pony tail and a ferret face smiled through his parted front teeth caked with bread. She fought bravely but he was able to pull her arms in back of her and tie them.

The man with the white beard opened his pants and pushed her to the ground. Her head hit a rock and she saw him opening his pants just before she became unconscious.

She had no idea what happened after that, how much time elapsed until one of the Gullah men found her as he searched the woods for herbs. He carried her to his home and called Lukas, who had returned from his meeting, and came for her immediately, bringing a doctor with him. She finally regained full consciousness. In the bed she could see semen and blood stains between her legs and she was in pain.

"It's all right, Eleanor. You'll be just fine. You're safe now."

She described the men as best she could, then turned into a fetal position. The doctor gave her a sedative.

"The shock. I don't think it's a serious concussion. Just keep an eye on her. As for the rape--treat her gently. It's a horrible act."

"Lukas, I need to speak with you aside," Colin said.

They went to the kitchen area.

"When Eleanor was a little girl she was abused by the man who was her so-called father. She wouldn't want you to know. But I'm tellin' you because it's goin' to take a much longer time than usual for her to recover from this. Her memories. The attacks were shameful and disgraceful, as you can imagine, and I never knew until later in her life or I swear I would have killed him."

Lukas clenched his fists.

"Good God, how much more can she take?"

"I'm afraid for her this time," Colin admitted.

The doctor appeared.

"She took the sedative. But keep an eye on her. She's awake now but will fall into a sleep soon. If she gets dizzy or throws up, call me immediately. Or if she feels a pain in her head. Much worse for her will be how she reacts to the rape. It is and will be a horror for her, which is a natural reaction. I'm going to give you a sedative I want you to give her for a few days and we'll take it from there to see how she reacts to what happened."

"I thank you, doctor."

After the doctor left, Lukas and Colin looked in on Eleanor who was fast asleep in a fetal position.

Lukas said, "I'll be right back."

He woke up Ed Colucci, Karl Ehrens, Dave Givens, and Matt Blank, his four most trusted men.

"It's Eleanor. She's been raped on St. Helena's. And this is to go no farther."

"Oh, Lord." Colucci was visibly upset. He thought the world of Eleanor.

"She said one man had a dirty-looking white beard and a red birthmark on his face and the other had a dirty blonde pony tail and parted teeth."

"Are Matt Carlson and Stevie Ripley at it again? I knew we should have cleaned out those woods. They been livin' there weeks now, ever since they got out of jail. Nobody's gonna hire two convicted felons just out of jail."

"You know what to do," Lukas said.

"Yes, boss. We will. That we will."

The four of them began to leave the room.

"Dirty bastards," Colucci mumbled.

"Let me know when it's finished," Lukas said.

Lukas McKendrick watched them entering the motor boat in the distance. He stood in agony, his heart beating erratically. Why had he let her go to St. Helena's alone? Was a God damned Tea Association meeting more important than Eleanor and her well being?

When would the time come, he wondered, when he would face things head on and tell her he was in love with her, that she had become the center of his life, above the tea plantation, which he never dreamed could occur. Tea and its production had been his life from childhood and his father had schooled him in the way of growing it. Now Eleanor had stepped into the picture. After this happened to her, he felt his heart had been even more intertwined with hers. Would it cause her to leave South Carolina and go back home? The clinic was pretty well finished. She could get some Gullah nurses trained to run it and go back to Paterson. The thought of that caused such an ache in his heart he felt it was breaking into bleeding shards and causing an excruciating pain in his chest.

He must convince her to stay. He must.

The men dressed quietly after Ed Colucci awakened them, went to the barn to get the supplies they needed. The night was dark; the stars were hardly visible and a heavy fog rose above the water. They knew they could not use any kind of lighting for their task or awaken anyone so they moved stealthily as they entered the boat that would take them to St. Helena's. After they landed on the island, they quietly searched the area's forest, past the giant old oaks, the pine trees, the dense shrubs. It seemed they were walking through blackness; but the moon gave them some light, and luckily a gasp of dawn would soon begin its rise.

They were about to give up when Matt Blank spotted Carlson and Ripley, hearing their loud snores. The men gathered together quietly, Colucci carrying the rope, plus a hammer if needed. The four of them stood over the two oblivious men. Then they attacked the felons before they knew what was happening. They fought them, finally able to wrestle them to the point of tying the rope they had brought around their hands which they had placed in back of them.

Colucci unwound the rest of the rope, threw it as high as he could over a heavy tree branch, then manipulated it until he had both ends in his hands, and created a noose. He grabbed Carlson, put it around his neck five times; the other men did the same to Ripley.

The felons cried out.

"Please! God, no. Please! No."

But the four kept to their task, lifted the two from the ground and strung them up. Their bodies quivered a few moments. Matt Blank cut the hanging ends of the two ropes.

They looked at the men swinging from the heavy tree limb. Their bodies had stopped quivering. It was over.

Colucci wrapped the part of the rope they did not use around his arm. He stared at the hanging bodies.

"That was for Eleanor," he said.

Then they left.

The sedative the doctor gave Eleanor did not help her sleep for a time. The incident at St. Helena's began her thinking of her childhood in Paterson, her so-called father's sexual abuse, her fears, the effect it had on her whole life. She thought of the severe depressions they caused her. And now this. If only she could see Dr. Brodsky she felt he would help her. Yet, she knew she must go on. The clinic for the Gullahs, the busyness of getting it in order would help her immensely. And then there was the quilting business she was helping Lula set up. No one knew of her past abuse in Paterson, she thought, except Colin, who would never speak a word. She began to feel sleepy. She saw Colin sitting by her bed. And Lukas had come in. He sat on the other side and took her hand. She saw tears running down his face. No. She would not let this good man and the others down. She must survive this.

Three days later Ed Colucci carried a newspaper in his hand and gave it to Lukas. The headline read TWO MEN FOUND HANGED IN ST. HELENA WOODS with photos of Matt Carlson and Steve Ripley. The police were questioning the Gullah community to see if they could get any information from them but so far they had no leads.

Lukas read the headline and article.

"You did a good job. They got what they deserved. It's just as well Eleanor not know so destroy that paper after you show it to Colin and tell him to keep quiet about it. I'm sure he'll agree."

Lukas rarely went into Charleston, but this time it was essential. He knocked on the door of Judge Jeremiah Jackson, a few minutes earlier than his appointment called for. He prayed his plan would work. Jackson was a mustached, white-haired man, the symbol of what the Old South aristocrats looked like as far as the appearance of its male population.

"Have a seat, sir." He gestured at a leather- covered chair placed in front of his desk.

"I don't believe we've ever met. I'm Lukas McKendrick."

They shook hands.

"The McKendrick that owns those hundreds of acres of tea plantations?"

"I'm afraid I'm guilty of that, sir," Lukas smiled.

"Now what can I do for you?"

"It's the case of the two men they found hanged in the woods of St. Helena's recently. I believe you've been appointed that case."

"I have."

"Those men, as you know, were former convicted felons. They'd been living in those woods for weeks. They had no prospects for a job with their records. I checked. No one would hire them. So I'm thinking maybe they committed suicide."

"Suicide? What proof have you got of that?"

"Just gut instinct."

"Well, once we find the men responsible, you may have a different thought about it."

"I don't want you to find the men responsible."

The judge raised his eyebrows.

"I don't understand."

"I'd consider it a suicide if I were you."

"You know, sir, I can't do that."

Lukas went into his pocket, brought out an envelope.

"Here's $25,000 that says you can. And you would be doing the world a favor with them out of it."

He put the envelope on the desk.

"Twenty-five thousand dollars!"

"That's right. That's what it's worth to me. And they would most likely be jailed again. And again. So what's the loss?"

"And what about justice, sir?"

"What I said is what I consider justice."

The judge looked at the envelope.

"You know you can go to prison for tryin' to bribe a judge?"

"I do, sir."

The judge did not speak for a time, then took the envelope and placed it in his pocket.

"Good day, sir."

"Good day, Judge Jackson."

Lukas had a smile on his lips most of the way home.

How true, he thought: Every man has his price.

In few months the clinic was finished. Eleanor, thankfully, was feeling stronger every day. She and Lukas were busy interviewing a few Gullah women she felt had potential with patients, women who were open to some of the new practices of medicine and newer medications about which she wanted to teach them. She finally hired Yvette Gunthers and Effie Shaw, who seemed most intelligent and likely to learn quickly. She also hired a part-time nurse, Elizabeth Swenson, who had excellent credentials, and a doctor, a young, idealistic fellow, Dr. Brandt, whose eyes still gleamed a bit when you referred to him as "doctor." She looked forward to every morning when one of the men, if not Lukas or her father, would take her over and stay for the day.

Part of the time she would also check on Lula who had sold two of her quilts and made two hundred dollars. She was ecstatic. Eleanor felt a sense of pride that she was part of Lula's success. She had finally brought her the sewing machine, teaching her how to use it. Now she was making even more quilts--and selling them now and then.

One day a surprising event occurred. Lukas approached her, red faced, twirling his hat.

"I wondered if you and Colin would like to come to dinner tomorrow night."

"We'd love to!"

Eleanor and Colin wondered, after all this time, why he had never invited them to dinner when she'd had him for dinner so often. She knew he was a loner because she noticed nobody else ever came to visit him as well.

"I thought I'd have Mattie make a Gullah dish since you seem so interested in their culture, as I am."

"How exciting! I can't wait!"

Lukas' living room was the size of her whole house. He was a gracious host, showing her what especially interested her, his collection of Gullah baskets on his wall, which surely must have numbered one hundred. Each of these sweet grass baskets had a different design interwoven into it. One was more beautiful than the other.

"How long have you been collecting them?"

She held up one of particular beauty in a pattern of sweet grass and a darker grass.

"For years. I don't even know how many. Are there any you particularly like? You can have them."

"Do you mean you'd be willing to give me part of your collection? I wouldn't hear of it. Besides," she smiled, "I've kind of started a collection of my own. I have five so far," she said proudly.

"Well, that's a wonderful beginning."

Mattie appeared.

"Dinner, suh."

She had made a one-pot stew, typical of Gullah cooking of rice, fresh cut up tomatoes, okra, shrimp, pork, chicken, carrots and seasoned to perfection with grits and gravy on the side.

Eleanor asked for the recipe.

"Don't mind if I have a second helping." Colin was also impressed.

For dessert they had watermelon tea and a vanilla cake.

After dinner they sat in the living room and talked mostly of the clinic and the tea crop this year.

Eleanor noticed the photograph of a beautiful woman with long black hair and soft brown eyes adorned by a silver frame on the coffee table. So that was why he never married. A lost love. He must have reminded himself every day when he looked at her photograph.

Time passed quickly, and the mantle clock soon chimed twelve.

"I guess we'd better be going," she offered. "A long day tomorrow. I'm going to show Yvette how to set a broken arm."

Lukas raised his eyebrows.

"You can do such a thing?"

Eleanor blushed. "I had a wonderful teacher, Dr. Mary Lafferty. I'm sorry to say she passed away. She left the Women's Alliance, the clinic in Paterson, to me, and I get weekly reports about how things are progressing there from Nora Pennington, a woman I appointed head nurse. I really do need to get back there and see for myself if things are going well."

Lukas knit his brow. "You wouldn't consider going back for good, would you?"

"I don't know. I do miss Paterson but I also love South Carolina. And I do know my father misses the mills."

"I hope and pray you decide to stay here. I--we--couldn't get along without you."

"Once Yvette and Effie are trained to my satisfaction at St. Helena's, then I suppose I'll decide."

They said their good nights. And that old familiar thrill shot through Lukas as he held her in his arms to say goodbye. All that lay within his heart, he realized, was torment at the thought she might leave.

The next day she looked out the window and saw an azure sky, a perfect day to air her quilts. She gathered them up and placed them on the clothes line to air. She was ready to go inside when she saw a man from far off walking up the road towards her house. She ran inside, pulled open the drawer of her dining room table, took the gun Lukas had taught her to use since the incident on St. Helena's and put it in her apron pocket.

As the man came closer, she thought she saw a familiarity in his gait. He had a beard and mustache, torn dungarees and dirty shoes. Yet, somehow he seemed to be someone she would recognize close up.

And as he approached the house, she knew she was right.

"Charles!"

She ran down the porch stairs and fell into his weak arms.

"What in God's name--Colin!"

They helped him up the stairs and brought him to the spare bedroom.

"How did you ever find me?"

"Nora Pennington--at the Alliance," he gasped. "She gave me your address. I've traveled to so many states, but I knew I had to come back--to you."

"Why are you here? I don't understand--"

He grasped his side.

"Eleanor--I'm dying. Please. Take me home. I want to die in Paterson."

Without hesitation, she answered.

"I will, Charles. I will."

Colin helped her undress him and put him to bed. She could see the weak condition he was in.

"We'll throw together a few things and leave tomorrow, Charles."

She knew time was precious.

She was packing when Lukas stopped by.

"And what are you packing for?"

"It's my ex-husband, Charles. He's dying and he wants to have his last breath and burial in Paterson, his home. I'll be away for a time."

"What can I do? Do you want me to go with you and Colin to help out?"

"No. I'm fine. Besides, you have too much to do here with the tea plants near coming to bud."

But she was not fine at all.

The next morning, having packed the necessities for the trip they set off.

Lukas stood watching the car disappearing into the distance until it looked the size of a post card.

He swallowed hard. It had come to him months ago he was desperately in love with Eleanor. But what right did an old fool in his late sixties have to profess his love to a young, beautiful girl? Suddenly, a feeling of terror seized him. What if she never came back? How could he ever go on? But, of course, she had to come back. Pathetic man, he thought. He knew she saw him as nothing but a friend. But no matter what the consequences, it came to him he should have professed his love. Yes. No matter what. His chance was tragically missed. He may have lost it if she didn't return. He felt as though his heart was crumbling. He punched the side of his house until he drew blood on his knuckles and tears in his eyes.

The pain in his chest came quickly. He grasped it with his right hand and fell to the ground. It was a few minutes later when Ed saw him lying on the ground, called the doctor, praying it was not too late.

"Eleanor," he moaned. "Get--Eleanor."

But that was an impossibility, for they were on the road to Paterson. And Ed felt despair for he had failed Lukas in the most important request he ever gave him.

The journey for Eleanor, Colin, and Charles was long and arduous for they were not as familiar with the roads as they should be. They slept in the car at night finding woods that appeared safe enough, Eleanor with her gun in her dress and Colin with his in his pocket until hotels appeared. It had been a terrifying experience for Eleanor as she remembered what had happened to her in the woods, but she dared not show it. As usual, she tried to look her calm, sensible self while inside of her deep fear lurked. Charles slept a great deal, which was a blessing.

When they reached Paterson, Eleanor's heart throbbed with joy. She had not realized how much she had missed it. She sensed Colin and Charles felt the same way. So many familiar sights bombarded her. But she must see the most familiar one, the Great Falls, in their eternal watchfulness. She stopped the car a minute or two to watch them in their splendor, as did Colin and Charles.

Charles had awakened since they'd entered Paterson. It was as though it was an omen that he be here.

When she arrived at her home, she saw Aaron on the porch reading the paper. Her heart performed somersaults at the sight of him, but she dared not show it and remained aloof.

"My God!" was all he could say when he looked up and recognized them.

"Aaron," she said coldly, "I'll explain everything later. Right now I need you and Colin to help Charles and bring him to the spare room."

"Of course!"

Eleanor carried in the baggage but they were too exhausted to unpack now.

"Of course, you can continue living here. I wasn't planning to throw you out in the street. But please don't speak to me unless you have to."

Eleanor had not really paid attention to Kirov with all the goings on, but now she could see as she looked at him he had lost a great deal of weight. His clothes seemed to hang upon him; his cheeks were sunken.

"As a doctor, Aaron, I need your help with Charles. Will you examine him and tell me what's what?"

"Certainly."

Kirov went for his medical satchel and examined Charles head to toe.

He decended the stairs slowly where Eleanor and Colin waited for his diagnosis.

"It doesn't look good. His lungs are hardly functioning. His liver from what I can tell, is nearly wasted away. His vital signs are practically non-existent. He needs to get to the hospital immediately."

"The hospital will do no good."

Eleanor told him his dying wish was to come back to Paterson. She knew it did not mean he wanted to come back to die in a hospital. "We'll make him as comfortable as we can here. I trust your judgment, Aaron. After all, you're a doctor. Do you think we're doing the right thing by letting him live these last days here instead of a hospital?"

Aaron hesitated, then said, "I do. As long as you are near him he will have more comfort and happiness here, I know, than any hospital. And I will monitor him constantly."

Eleanor stared at Kirov.

He had not said this with jealousy or malice in his voice. Instead, she heard compassion.

Eleanor spent the next few days with Charles as much as possible. He seemed semi-conscious most of the time, but she felt certain he could hear her. She spoke to him for her own relief as well as his.

"Do you remember when I first met you? Poor, starving waif that I was during the strike. And you gave me food. And the carousel. Remember--we went to Palisades Amusement Park? I can honestly say that was one of the best times I ever had. And the garden. Do you remember our wonderful after-dinner walks in the garden surrounded by those magnificent flowers? And the films we went to? Such laughter! And," she took his hand, "the day you proposed. Charles, I hope you can hear me. You gave me some of the happiest times of my life."

"Many happy memories. "

She stared into space.

She turned to Charles, saw a slight smile on his face, and then his eyes closed.

She took his pulse.

He was dead.

Charles was buried at Holy Sepulcher Cemetery, beside his mother, father, sister Mary, and a few feet from baby Robbie's grave. The day was crisp and autumn leaves had begun to fall. She could hear the trilling of the larks in the distance and starlings fluttering in nearby trees; as it turned out, his grave lay close to a giant maple which hovered over it, a fitting place for a man who loved nature so. The light blue sky was filled with cumulus clouds which scudded across it.

She stood, silent in her grief, grateful she would always have memory to sustain her.

Colin and Aaron stood like sentinels next to her, along with a few hundred workers, mostly from the mills and many of the owners who knew him.

The priest read from the Mass for the Dead.

"And Lord," he said, "Will he who believes in you rise on the third day and with thee?" "He will," Jesus said.

"At that time Martha said to Jesus, "Lord, if Thou hadst been here my brother would not have died. But even now I know that whatever Thou shalt ask of God, God will give it to Thee." Jesus said to her, "Thy brother shall rise." Martha said to Him, "I know that he will rise at the resurrection on the last day." Jesus said to her, "I am the resurrection and the life; he who believes in me shall never die. Dost thou believe this?" She said to Him, "Yes, Lord, I believe Thou art the Christ, Son of God, Who has come into the world."

Charles was a believer but always said he did not want a formal service for his burial. "All that pomp," he used to say. But Eleanor felt she wanted to say something that Charles might feel appropriate to speak at his passing. She thought of one of his favorite writers, Henry Scott Holland, and decided she would speak one of Charles' favorite quotations from his writings. Her legs felt like water; her heart was beating wildly, but she must do this for Charles' sake. She stepped forward towards the grave, felt someone taking her arm to help her, to see her through. It was Aaron.

She began the passage Charles loved so:

Death is nothing at all. It does not count. I have only slipped away into the next room. Nothing has happened. Everything remains exactly as it was. I am I and you are you, and the old life that we lived so fondly together is untouched, unchanged. Whatever we were to each other, that we are still. Call me by the old familiar name. Speak of me in the easy way which you always used. Put no difference into your tone. Wear no forced air of solemnity or sorrow. Laugh as we always laughed at the little jokes that we enjoyed together. Play, smile, think of me, pray for me. Let my name be ever the household word that it always was. Let it be spoken without an effort, without the ghost of a shadow upon it. Life means all that it ever meant. It is the same as it ever was. There is absolute and broken continuity. What is this death but a negligible accident? Why should I be out of mind because I am out of sight? I am but waiting for you, for an interval, somewhere very near, just around the corner. All is well. Nothing is hurt; nothing is lost. One brief moment and all will be as it was before. How we shall laugh at the trouble of parting when we meet again!

Before leaving, each mourner placed a rose on Charles' casket. She heard the sound of earth, its dull impact from a spade burying the coffin.

Her walk was unsteady when the ritual was over and she was glad Aaron and Colin stood by her side to hold her up and lead her to the car. She could not help but wonder that perhaps she could have saved him by her love, that he would still be alive.

Neither Aaron, Colin or Eleanor spoke on the drive home.

Two weeks later, Eleanor was accompanied by Colin to Charles' attorney's office, Grimes and Grimes, to read his will. As he had once told her, he left all he possessed to Eleanor. She had risen from near starvation and poverty in a tenement to becoming a woman of great wealth.

But what did it matter?

Charles was gone....

She knew immediately what she must do. She could hardly move her limbs to get out of bed. She called Dr. Brodsky, her psychiatrist. Colin drove her and waited in the car as she slowly and carefully walked to his office.

He hadn't changed a bit. Same chubby build and kind look in his eyes.

"I needed to see you. My ex-husband, Charles, died," she said, her voice threadbare.

And then all the pain and tears she had held back for so long burst forth, for it was safe to be herself here. Brodsky put his arms around her and let her cry herself out.

After a time, she gained some semblance of composure.

"I feel such guilt. If he hadn't met me on that fated day and met some other woman, most likely he would be alive now and living happily ever after. Instead, he chose me." She burst into tears again. "And I feel largely responsible for his death. I've said this to no one, of course, but it haunts me day and night."

"So you have a crystal ball that tells you these things?"

"Don't make fun of me."

"I assure you I am not. This is very serious. But you must understand, Eleanor, the role of fate, of coincidence in our lives. You gave him so much happiness for so much of the time. And he loved you to distraction. How many men can say that in a relationship with a woman? This is a beautiful thing. For the time that you had the relationship was good and I'm sure any pain was worth it to him because of his overwhelming love for you. Are you forgetting he sacrificed his own happiness so that you could go forward and find yours? Focus on the happiness you had during your time together, not the sorrow. I'm sure he did. Will you promise me that?"

"I--I'll try."

"Eleanor you are a depressive and every day of your life you must concentrate on not falling back into that low state again. You've survived so much, starting with your childhood abuse. And that's what life is. Survival. However, I don't think you are at the point you need to go back to Red Stone Asylum again."

"God, please, no."

"Then you must work very hard on improving yourself, being more positive, every day."

"I'll try. I'll try with all my might."

She sighed, bereft of emotion which had stripped her bare.

"Let's change the subject. Tell me about your life on the tea plantation. Was it helpful to you?"

"Oh, yes, in many ways. Except for one incident I'm not ready to talk about."

"As you say."

"Well, the fresh air, although it got so hot at times, the fascination of the tea creation, the lovely dinner the owner had for us. He is the kindest elderly man, and he watched over me. He owned the plantation."

"It sounds wonderful. But complicated. Since you liked South Carolina as well as Paterson, you will have to choose where you will be living."

"That's on my mind constantly as well. I helped start a clinic there for the poor so I've got to go back to be sure it's running well. I think the two girls I chose to run it will be just fine. It's on one of the islands, St. Helena, where the poorer part of the colored population live. I want to enlarge it, and the one in Paterson as well."

"I should have known you would do such a thing."

"Charles left me a great deal of money and I think it would be a wonderful memorial to him."

"There are a few other important issues we must address next time, your stillborn baby as well as your relationship with Aaron Kirov."

"I don't want to talk about those things. I'll settle them myself." He frowned.

"If I'm right, you haven't settled them so far. You have tucked them away in your heart and mind and you must talk about them, as painful as it will be."

He glanced at the clock on the desk.

"I'll see you again, say, Saturday at eleven o'clock."

"Yes. That would be fine."

She had no intention of going back.

A few weeks later they packed and readied to return to South Carolina again. Although Colin never said a word, he was very unhappy at the thought of going back. Paterson was his home; weaving and loom fixing his trade. And he hated the heat of the South. Lukas had been more than generous in paying him for his work on the tea plantation, but it was just not the same as weaving and loom fixing. And his hopes were not fulfilled. He wanted Eleanor and Aaron to reunite and genuinely thought they would, but it did not happen. She was living in, it seemed to him, the same state of mind she felt when she left Paterson the last time. He had hoped Dr. Brodsky would help her see the light, but that did not happen. She was supposed to see him the day before yesterday, according to the calendar on her wall. But that did not happen. He knew that most likely if he gave Eleanor feedback that he wanted her to stay in Paterson, she would listen, though in the long run he felt it must be her choice.

Eleanor had hardly spoken to Kirov since she had returned and only when necessary. She knew he was suffering from their estrangement as much as she was; yet, she could not bring herself to forgive him. Each time she saw him her heart fractured, but her stubborn attitude prevailed. She hated herself for loving him so completely and being unable to say the words, "I forgive you."

The journey to South Carolina turned out to be a more relaxed trip than the semi-frantic one they had taken with Charles lying in the back seat of the car near death. She breathed in the fresh air and felt exhilarated as they drove down the road which would eventually lead them to the tea plantation and Lukas. She was even more grateful it was coming close to the end of the tea picking season and would not be so hectic. Still, a quiet hovered over the place which gave Eleanor a sense of foreboding.

Ed greeted her with a sorrowful look upon his face. She had not expected to see him but rather Lukas who would hold her in his arms and greet her at returning.

Ed gave her a hug which seemed a bit too formal.

"Miss Eleanor, I got the worse news you can imagine. Lukas. He died. He died last Thursday on the 24th."

She fainted, woke up on the couch in her living room.

"His heart, you know. He never watched his health. Heart attack. It was six years ago he was told he had a bad heart and he never went to the doctor since." Ed shuffled his hat in his hands. "He never listened. The plantation and all the work it took must of caught up with him."

"Lukas. Dead?" was all Eleanor could respond. "If only Colin and I could have come sooner. I could have paid my respects, gone to his funeral."

She pulled out her handkerchief and wept, her grief inconsolable, her heart thumping so much it almost hurt.

"You were on the road when it happened. There was no way to contact you. It was a small service. He always said he wanted to be cremated and his ashes placed near the gigantic pine tree you see when you enter St. Helena's forest. And that's just what we did."

"His last word was your name."

"Oh, God..."

She hugged her body hard.

"At least he didn't suffer long."

She clenched her temples and felt the signs of a migraine headache beginning.

"This can't be true. It can't! And what happiness did he really have besides the plantation? Strange he never had any visitors. And his lost love. That didn't come to pass either."

"Lost love?"

"Yes. The picture he has on his coffee table of the beautiful woman with black hair and kind brown eyes."

"Oh, that wasn't his sweetheart, Miss Eleanor. That was his mother. You see, Lukas was half Gullah. That's why we never had any visitors. Whites would never come here and eat at the same table with a colored man, would never socialize with a man who had Gullah blood."

Eleanor could have been blown away like a flake of dust.

"Why, that's despicable."

Suddenly, with all the news that had bombarded her, her body seemed not able to function. She went to her bed and stayed there all the next day while Colin brought her breakfast and dinner. She ate little. The next day she forced herself to get out of bed and lay on the sofa in the living room. She was totally cried out. First Charles. Now Lukas. The pain she felt was too deep for tears.

The next morning she placed a spoon and a bottle of water in her hand bag. At 6 a.m. she woke up Ed Colucci and asked him if he would take her in the boat to the cremation site. Of course, he obliged. When they arrived, the fog was lifting. She asked him to please go down river twenty minutes or so, for she wanted to be completely alone with Lukas' remains. He did as she asked. When she could hardly see Ed in the distance, she stood beneath a mourning sky, then took a tablespoon and performed the sacred act of gathering together a spoon of the crematory remains which, thankfully, had not yet blown away. She stared at them; they were the lightest pink. She placed the tablespoon in her mouth, washed them down with some of the water she had brought with her. She did this three times as a sacred act of love.

"Now you will always be a part of me, Lukas. Always. I love you dearly. Goodbye, dear friend."

She stood staring at what was left of the remains for quite a few minutes before Ed Colucci returned.

She got in the boat with him.

Neither spoke on the way back.

She knew Lukas would want her to gather herself together and resume the life she knew. And she slowly did just that. The Gullah clinic was on her mind; and now, more than ever, she wanted it to be finished and bear Lukas' name as a memorial to him. She also wanted to set up Lula better with her quilt business and provide fabric and supplies for her, perhaps hire one of the Gullah women to help her.

"There was a sudden measles epidemic," Ed informed her. He looked at her with admiration. "All those pages and pages of directions you gave to Yvette and medical books on how to treat all kinds of illnesses if her herbal remedies didn't work--she followed them. They did the trick. We think some tourist to the island must have been carrying the virus or whatever it's called, and that's how it started."

A week later she and Colin set out again for St. Helena. When they arrived, they were greeted by Yvette.

"So sad about Mr. McKendrick. We went to the service and cried and cried. He was good to us."

"Yes, he was. Yvette, I want to speak to you privately."

They went to her home, clean and neatly furnished. Granny afghans everywhere as well as quilts added lively color to the room, along with the beautiful baskets she had created.

"I want to put you formally in charge of the clinic. I'll pay you $25 more a week."

"$25 dollars! That way too much."

"No, it isn't. It's a lot of responsibility. Besides, I want to share the wealth I've come into for worthy causes. And I want you to select one other woman, train her, and have her act as nurse when needed at the clinic. Pick the most intelligent one, of course--perhaps Effie--if you agree, and one with a kind heart. You can't really be a good nurse unless you have a sympathetic heart. I don't want someone who thinks of it only as a job," she warned, "because she will be dealing with human life."

"And the quilts. I want you to encourage Lula to keep making them. They are works of art. Perhaps she can teach another girl to help her. I can see them on display in a museum some day. I really can. In fact, I wrote to a museum in New York about them and their background."

"Oh Lawd. And will you be near if we need you?"

"I really don't know yet whether I'll go back to Paterson or stay here."

"I hope you stay, Miss Eleanor."

"I'll surely come back one way or another from time to time to see how things are working out. But more and more I'm feeling I want to go back to my roots in Paterson, where I truly belong, especially with Lukas gone."

"We gonna miss yuh."

Lunch time arrived and Yvette insisted she and Colin stay. They were happy to oblige. She prepared a salmon pie with various spices and green tea with home made biscuits.

"We always say the Gullah Lord's Prayer before we eat. I hope you don't mind."

"Of course not."

Yvette clasped her hands together, as they did, and spoke the prayer:

We Fada wa dau sen heshen
Leb ebrybody hona ya name
We pray dat soon ya gwine rule oba de wol.
Wasoneba ting ya wan
Leh um be so een dis wol

Same like dey een heaven.
Gu we de food wa we need
Dis dayyah an ebry day.
Fagibe we fa we sin
Same like we da fagibe dem people
Wa do bad ta we.
Leh we doh hab hand test
Wen Satan try we
Keep we from ebil.

This was the first time Eleanor and Colin heard the true Gullah language and they were fascinated by it.

Eleanor and Colin felt a sense of contentment knowing Yvette was willing to be head nurse for she trusted her completely. Colin was secretly thrilled that Eleanor's mind seemed to be leading towards the direction of going back to Paterson.

They stayed an hour or so, mostly discussing clinical procedures, the quilts, plus addresses Yvette needed to know to get her supplies. She also gave her her address and phone number in Paterson where she could be reached.

"I think we'd better get goin'," Colin offered. "It looks overcast and you don't want to be caught in a storm. That's for sure."

They said their goodbyes amidst tears and arrived at the tea plantation before the storm hit.

Eleanor watched the crying rain pelting upon her window glass of her bedroom window, quiet in her sorrow. What direction would her life take now? Certainly she would not miss the terrifying hurricanes of South Carolina, and with Lukas gone what sense was there in staying? She was certain of only one thing, her love of Paterson. And what of Kirov? She still loved him with a passion she could barely endure when he was near her. But, yet, she could not speak. Only one person could help her out of her dilemma and untangle her mind. And that was Dr. Brodsky.

They arrived in Paterson after a long, arduous drive. The third day she made an appointment with Dr. Brodsky. He entered his office with a frown on his face when he saw her.

"You did not keep your last appointment and I did not hear from you."

"Please forgive me. So much has happened."

"All the reason you should be keeping your appointments."

"I promise I will from now on."

"Lukas, the wonderful man I told you ran the tea plantation, died. Charles, my ex-husband, is dead as well. I'm putting on a smiling face; but I don't want to go on anymore; yet, I know I must."

"That you do not continue with your life is not an option. Do you understand?"

She paused a few moments.

"Yes, I understand. I have too many obligations to other people."

"Another thing has traumatized me deeply and I wasn't ready to talk about it before. I was raped when I was at St. Helena's Island. It was brutal and horrible." She clenched her hands. "It brought back so many memories of my being abused in childhood I wasn't able to function a time."

"Good God, no wonder you are in states of severe depression. But I must tell you, Eleanor, the way to defeat this is to live for today as much as you can. Today only. Make the very best you can of each day for none of us knows what lies ahead. Think that instead of talking of the past we must think of today and the future. You know, Kirov is near breakdown from this estrangement."

She realized then, as she guessed, he must be seeing Brodsky as well.

"The miscarriage. I feel perhaps in his heart Kirov blames me for the baby's death. After all, I carried her" She began to weep. "My darling baby girl. She was so beautiful."

"Concerning Kirov, you could not be further from the truth. And, once again, we are dealing with the past."

"I have dreams about the baby. Grotesque dreams. When will they ever stop?"

"When you accept what happened as part of the past. There is no reason you cannot have normal, healthy children. As I have heard (from Kirov she knew), the baby was born with a cord around her neck. So tragic. But also so rare. Did you know that?"

"No, I didn't."

"Well, as a doctor, I am telling you this now."

"And who will I have my next child with, a stranger?"

"You will have it with Kirov if you follow my advice."

"And what is that?"

"I want you to speak to Nora and Brigitte."

"Never."

"They have been wanting to talk to you for a long time; but, of course, you ignore Brigitte completely."

"I will never speak with them about this topic."

"Since you don't plan to follow my advice, I think it best to end our sessions."

Eleanor gasped.

"Oh, please. No. I need you."

"How can you say that if you don't follow what I tell you?"

"This is partially Kirov's idea, isn't it? I'm sure he's seeing you."

"I have no comment on that. But either you follow my advice and we make an appointment for your next visit or walk out of my office now. For good."

She did not speak for a time, heard the seconds ticking away on the clock on his wall.

"Could you give me an appointment in a few weeks? I received a letter saying I must go to South Carolina to hear Lukas' will read."

"Wednesday at ten in three weeks? Is that good or you? By then I would expect you spoke with Brigitte and Nora."

"Yes."

"You know, Eleanor, a relationship with a psychiatrist is based on trust. I'm glad you have come to the conclusion to trust my advice. Remember, you must continue to replace anger and hatred with understanding and forgiveness. It is the only way to survive as a completely human being."

"But what if I can't?" She clenched her forehead with her hands. "The hurt is so deep."

"Of course you can. I only ask that you give it a chance."

"I don't know if I can."

He smiled at her.

"But I know that you can."

"I'm confused and fearful of forgiveness. It may mean weakness."

"On the contrary, it is a sign of strength. And, alas, we are all fearful to an extent. That is why the world is in the state it's in."

"What should I do?"

"You must also speak with Kirov as well as Brigitte and Nora to find out what happened. And perhaps why."

"I know what happened."

"But was it completely his fault?"

"Of course."

"I have a feeling it was more complicated than you think."

"I'll--think--about speaking with them."

"Good. We are progressing."

"I'll call you as soon as I return from South Carolina."

"I hope so."

"You may be sure of it."

She smiled at him as she left the office.

The next next day Eleanor called Brigitte into her office and closed the door. Brigitte was trembling all over.

"I knew the day would come, Miss Eleanor, when you would fire me. And I can't say that I blame you."

"And what do you mean by that?"

"I've been wanting to tell you for weeks. It's my fault--what happened."

"I expect a full explanation for all of this."

"Well, it started out when I first saw Dr. Kirov. He was so handsome. From the minute I saw him, I developed a crush on him. Well," she took a handkerchief out of her pocket and blew her nose in it, tears streaming down her face. "Not as much now that he's turning to skin and bones and he's so pale." She began to cry. "And it's all my fault. I'm the one who watched him for weeks and developed such an attraction to him I couldn't contain myself. And I know, being a man with his wife pregnant, he would be more vulnerable. And I was right. I have to emphasize to you that he never even glanced at me that first day except for a nice hello. I began to talk to him more and more and was thrilled when he answered me back. And then that terrible day I led him to the basement. But I want you to know I started it, that it's all my fault. All of it."

"Not all of it."

"But I led him on. He spoke about you and this was the worst thing he could do to hurt you. But--sexually--" she blushed, "he seemed starved if you don't mind me saying it so bluntly. Ahhhh," she sighed. "I'm so glad this is off my chest and I'm ready for the consequences of being fired."

"Brigitte, I'm so glad I heard your story. You straightened some things out for me. I can see them more clearly now. And, of course, you can stay. You are a wonderful nurse."

Brigitte blew her nose in her handkerchief again.

Eleanor placed her arms around her.

"Now, now, as someone recently told me this is all part of the past. It's the future we have to think about. Will you call in Nora for me?"

Nora entered hesitantly, looking efficient, as she always did, in her starched cotton dress, her watch dangling from its chain on her belt. Eleanor sensed immediately she was correct putting her in charge.

"Well, Nora, what can you tell me about what happened with my husband and Brigitte?"

"I'm glad you finally asked me, Miss Eleanor. I was afraid to approach you about it. I noticed for months Brigitte had a crush on Dr. Kirov. But I swear he tried to avoid her at all costs. When you got pregnant, she seemed more and more, well, I wouldn't say aggressive but attentive to him, touching his arm and the like. And that's when it started. A few months after you got pregnant. But I swear to you Dr. Kirov avoided her like the plague a long time."

"I'm glad you told me this. I should have spoken to you a long time ago. Thank you, Nora."

Colin kept his thoughts to himself, not wanting to upset Eleanor. He knew she had enough on her mind. But these trips to South Carolina were taking more of his stamina than he expected. And with that thought in mind, he worried about Eleanor as well. What would happen to her if he died? He could not bear the thought of her going through life alone when she could have someone as wonderful as Kirov by her side throughout life. And there could be children. Dr. Birnbaum had assured him of that. But he did not speak to her. She must resolve these problems herself. He knew she felt the same passion for Kirov as she had when they first met; he could see it every time Kirov and she were in the same room. But still, stubbornness ruled. He knew, alas, she received that trait from him.

The trip down to South Carolina took more out of both of them, this time largely with the thought of Lukas' death hovering over them. The one saving grace was that everything was in bloom, magnolia trees especially.

Eleanor was stunned when she heard Lukas' will. He left her 50% profits from the tea plantation, the other half to go to Ed Colucci, his faithful friend and supervisor for thirty years. He also left his home and plantation to Colucci. If Eleanor decided to live in South Carolina, however, his home would go to her.

Ed approached her after the will was read.

She could hardly speak she was in such shock.

The tea plantation profits. Those, along with the money Charles left her, made her an extremely wealthy woman, probably one of the wealthiest in Paterson.

She finally gained control of herself.

"I think everything should remain the same, Ed. I'll visit from time to time--I have the clinic and the quilt business to think of--and if I'm not down here, you can send me a check for the profits of the tea sales as they occur. I hope that makes sense."

"I can't believe it, Miss Eleanor. I never dreamed--"

"Lukas knew he had a good man in you and wanted to reward you. But me--?"

"Don't you know he was in love with you, from the first time he laid eyes on you, I think. You gave him the happiest times of his life, and I bless you for it."

"In love with me? Lukas?" She squeezed her temples. "How could I have been so blind?"

'Well, I can see why you wouldn't think it. He knew he was half Gullah after all, and, of course there was the age difference."

"I wish I would have known. I would have been kinder to him."

"You couldn't be any kinder than you was. It couldn't have been no different."

"I suppose you're right," she conceded.

In love with her. Eleanor thought about it most of the way driving home. When she told Colin, he said he suspected it all along. But they'd had a wonderful friendship and his ashes would remain a secret part of her. She was glad of that. She also thought about her conversation with Dr. Brodsky over and over again. She shivered at the thought of facing Kirov. But Brodsky was right. It must be done. When they arrived home, she and Colin plopped into bed, and Colin slept until ten in the morning. He had breakfast and went with Ed to the fields.

Eleanor was still not completely sure she would stay in Paterson. She decided her best move would be to explore the city, get the feel of it again, to see if this was truly the place where she wanted to spend the rest of her life. She was up at eight o'clock, donned a plain brown dress and tie shoes and socks to fit in better with the people in the parts of the city she planned to visit.

Her first stop was at the mill where she worked as a very young girl.

A tall man, ferret faced, with decayed teeth that showed through a kind smile and large hands, greeted her.

"May I help you, ma'am?"

"I--used to work here. I wonder if I could look around. It would mean a great deal to me."

"I don't see why not."

The first change she noticed was that there were only eight instead of ten workers dipping the silk at the tubs, removing the neatsfoot oil, lifting it up and down, up and down. This surprised her.

She went upstairs, surprised to see two of the weaving machines were vacant, and the same was true of the ribbon workers' machines, in contrast to the constant busyness on the floor when she was there.

"What's happened? When I was here, every machine was whirring away."

"Well, things have slowed down. Overall, output in the country is down nearly ten per cent and one fifth of the labor force in general's out of work if the papers are right. I think they are based on the slowdown I've seen here. Then, of course, some of them left to try to start their own shop, paid the boss for their machine, then are payin' him back. But they can work as long as they want. I think it's a lousy idea myself. Lots of the workers get sick, exhausted."

"But what about the unions? Can't they do anything?"

"We have a different union now, the ASW, the Associated Silk Workers. There was just another strike, for fourteen weeks, which was successful under the leadership of the ASW. Against Johnson- Cowdin Company trying to reinstitute the forty eight hour week." The foreman frowned. "And, of course, some workers just got sick and tired of strikes and moved to other places. Most likely Pennsylvania. They say the working conditions are better there, but that's only a rumor 'sfar as I know."

"I haven't kept up with what's been happening with the unions here; I've been away a lot. But it looks like nothing much has changed regarding Paterson and strikes."

"Right you are. Like the song says."

"What song is that?"

"You must surely know it: "Ain't We Got Fun.""

"Some of it from the radio."

"I was thinkin' of the part that says, "In the winter, in the summer/Don't we have fun?/ Times are bum and getting bummer/ Still we have fun.""

"And the worst of all is they're tryin' to replace silk."

"Replace silk? That's impossible."

"They're moving along. Five, ten years I don't even know if the mills will exist. I get the journal **Silk Today**, the Bible of the silk industry, and read a very scary article about what's down the pike. A chemist at DuPont is working on what they call a synthetic polymer--some name like that--and is tryin' to produce a melted polymer you can stretch out into strings of fiber. They are tryin' to create the first synthetic silk which the chemists call superpolyester. If they do, that's it for the silk mills in Paterson. It's part of my job to keep up with these things."

Eleanor felt shaken to the core.

"I don't believe it. Nothing can replace silk. People won't want it."

"Well, like I said, it's still in the experiment stage. But it doesn't look good for the silk mills if they succeed."

She observed the workers standing, eating their lunches. So little seemed to be different, better, as far as working conditions. As she was leaving, she passed the machine where she had rescued her friend, Katherine, who had betrayed her in the worst possible way.

She thought of Dr. Brodsky's words and turned to leave.

"Thank you for letting me look around."

"My pleasure."

She left fighting a state of depression; her heart felt splintered in pieces, attempting to think of the present, the future, as Dr. Brodsky had advised.

She decided to go to the tenement where she had lived as a young girl. A kind-looking woman with rosy, round cheeks, rather obese, and two children with red hair and snotty noses let her in.

Memories flooded over her--her so-called "father's" abuse, reading with her mother, the coal stove burning away as they hovered over it in winter, the paint peeling from the ceilings and walls, the same cot she laid on night after night, its stuffing coming out, the tack holes in the walls where her flower paintings had been, Charles sitting at the table having tea and strawberry jam and her shame at her poverty, his carrying her mother up the icy stairs when she was so sick, the puppy he gave her, their trip to Palisades Amusement Park, the first time she could remember when she was truly happy--then his steep decline into alcoholism and his leaving her to give her a chance at true happiness.

"It's not much but it's all we can afford. And now there's talk of another strike. God knows how we'll get through it."

Eleanor opened her purse and gave her twenty dollars.

"Oh, my God! Bless you. I can get some groceries with this."

"I know what life was like her first hand. Would you mind if I look at the porch?" "Of course not."

She stood in the doorway of the porch and remembered Dante sitting with her on the wicker sofa, still there, and her declaration of love to him. She thought of his dynamic speeches in the building on Fair Street, his arms reaching to heaven, the first time he spoke with her on the bench near the Great Falls, her being reunited with him in Bayonne and their passionate desires finally fulfilled, then his leaving her for Russia and never contacting her again. What had become of him? She would never know.

She decided to go to Silk Road and the Victorian house where she and Charles had lived during much of their marriage. She thought of happy times when Charles would return from the mill, and they would walk through the garden, sharing the day's events, examining the glorious flowers. She thought of her life with her beloved son, Robbie, who died of diphtheria. Images passed before her of Robbie in his sailor suit and his first pair of shoes, propped on Charles' lap, Charles constantly hugging and kissing him. And there was the memory of Katherine, who was largely responsible for Robbie's death, and then her suicide. She remembered her running from her home to Bayonne, to meet Dante, who was her great love then. She decided not to attempt to enter the house. The agony of memory was too deep.

She decided to visit the Women's Alliance. Nora and Brigitte greeted her; Nora hugged her hard.

"We really can't wait until you come back," Nora said. "There's so many more out of work now, and sick."

"I'm going to make a lot of changes, enlarge the Alliance a great deal. It will be very different from what it is now. Much larger. Perhaps a hospital. Even if I decide to stay in South Carolina that will happen. I have to find a large piece of property for it--so much else will need to be done." She smiled. "But it will be well worth it." She walked around, saw so many people suffering, some in beds on the floor.

Then, as difficult as it was for her, she entered Mary's office. She saw a vision of her sitting at her office desk, thought of the strife they had gone through during the flu epidemic, her idolizing Mary so, and then her death of breast cancer. She thought of Mary's last moments when she held her in her arms. And it was then that she decided the hospital she planned to have built would be named after Mary.

She left the Women's Alliance, walking through the alley where her mother had been attacked and later died. She remembered with disgust Angus Clegg who had tried to rape her as well.

Then she walked across the Broadway Bridge, paused, studied the Passaic River a time, shimmering like gold from the sun's reflection, to Holy Sepulcher Cemetery and peered through its gate. She thought of her mother, Mary, Charles, and her child, Robbie, all buried there, alone in the darkness.

She finally walked to the one place that gave her peace, the Great Falls. They gushed in their full splendor, their deafening sound permeating her overwrought heart and soul, its droplets touching her face. She sat down on the bench she had once shared with Dante and watched the falls for a long time. She thought too of Aaron as he administered to patients at the Alliance, his psychiatric knowledge saving Ann Dodge, his survival after the fire at the asylum, which took his wife's life, her own great love and desire for him she thought could never come to her again after Dante. But it did.

Suddenly, she thought of Dr. Brodsky. Like a bolt of lightning his words came back to her: "You must stop living in the past. Live in the moment, and above all, learn forgiveness." And what had she been doing? Letting the past be her constant companion, remembering a time that was gone, would never return. And in that moment she knew where she belonged.

Home.

Eleanor's heart began pounding when she arrived home, watching Kirov eating his dinner, which he had prepared for himself since she had refused to do anything for him.

She took a deep breath.

"Aaron, I think it's time for us to talk. It should have been much sooner than now. I've noticed how thin you've become, and I hope it's not because of our estrangement, though I'm sorry to say I think that's part of it."

His hands began to tremble as he put down his fork, did not answer.

"Dr. Brodsky has suggested we talk and I think he's right."

"I'm seeing him too you know. I could no longer bear the pain of not talking this out with someone, of not speaking to you, of not holding you."

"I spoke to Brigitte and Nora about what happened. Now I want to hear your side of the story."

"As I've mentioned, Brigitte had been making advances to me for quite a time; in fact, since I started working at the Women's Alliance. Nora Pennington, I believe, will also testify to that if you ask her. She was not happy about it for Brigitte sometimes got distracted from her work when I was around. I in no way encouraged her. And," he blushed, "with you pregnant and your desire not to have sex during your pregnancy--I think it is more of a man's need for sex than a woman, though I know of no studies on such things--I turned to Brigitte."

"I understand better now. I believe you. I was very fearful of sex then. That was my fault completely. I didn't realize the seriousness of the situation. I thought perhaps you had fallen in love with her."

He rose from the table, kissed her passionately. She felt her emotions permeating her body as they had not for a long time.

"I could never love any woman as much as I love you."

It took all her strength to push him away.

"There are some other things I must talk with you about. I've inherited half of Lukas McKendrick's tea plantation profits, though I swear to you I never slept with him. I'm an unbelievably wealthy woman now. And I know exactly what I want to do with the money. I'm hoping you'll agree. I remembered that building on Mill Street where a silk mill closed down. Now it's vacant. I want to refurbish it, make it into a hospital and name it after Mary. I want you to have a psychiatrist's office there as well. I now realize what a good psychiatrist can do to help heal a patient. A hospital like this has always been my dream. The Alliance where we are now is cramped with beds on the floor, as you know. We constantly have to turn away patients. And I'm going to establish one on St. Helena's Island, off the coast of South Carolina, as well."

She folded her arms across her chest.

"Well, what do you think?"

"I'm practically speechless. I think it would be wonderful."

"Good! I'll need your input on what we'll need and how we'll put it together. We have to get architects to set up plans and so much else must be done."

He held her in his arms. They clung to each other like the roots do to a tree, giving it sustenance.

"This is a new beginning, Eleanor. I can feel it."

"Yes. I feel it too."

"I've got to get over to St. Joseph's. I'm late already. But," he smiled, "we will continue discussing this tonight, I assure you."

That evening Colon, Aaron and Eleanor sat on the wicker rocking chairs on the porch. Colin pretended to yawn.

"I'm exhausted. Going to bed early."

He knew when it was time to leave them alone.

The sky was a dark blue pane of glass, dazzling stars glittering through it here and there, the moon full and bright, its light shining down upon them. Aaron moved his rocking chair closer to her, held her hand. She felt as much a part of him as her breath.

She thought of how much she had survived. It took a special kind of courage to confront the pain and suffering she had known in her life, though she did not realize it. They sat, absorbing the silence of the night. She heard the sound of the radio in the house, playing one of her favorite songs:

Just a song at twilight, when the lights are low,
And the flick'ring shadows softly come and go,
Tho' the heart be weary, sad the day and long,
Still to us at twilight comes Love's old song....
Footsteps may falter, weary grow the way,
Still we can hear it at the close of day,
So til the end, when life's dim shadows fall,
Love will be found the sweetest song of all.

She smiled at Aaron, then gazed at the dazzling sky, heard the quietude of the endless heavens, a peacefulness permeating her. Life lay ahead with all its sorrows. And its joys. But one thing she knew for certain.

She would endure.

BIBLIOGRAPHY

I owe a great debt to those writers whose books and research were so helpful and inspirational and wish to acknowledge them and their work.

Danielson Krissi. Abouthealth, http://miscarriage.about. com/of/immediatemedicalconcerns/p/stillbirth/httm. about.com

Arts Midwest World Fest. P. 1 W http://artsmidwestorg/about

Baby Center Advisory Board, "Understanding Stillbirth"

Bernstein Paula, M.D., Ph.D. p1 "Pregnancy Complications", ww.babycenter.com/pregnancy-complications

Bergen Record, Aug. 10, 2014, "Remembering Emma," p. 14 Bigelow, Davis C. "My Mother Loved Tea," Canada, Benjamin Press, 2008, reprinted 2009, 2011

Bigelow Davis, Charleston Tea Plantation: America's Tea Garden, video, www. Charlestonteaplantation.com

Cannon, Gwen. Must Sees: Charleston, Savannah and the South

Carolina Coast, Great Britain, London, Michelin, Apa, 2009

Conserve Energy Future--"Hurricanes" -----"Hurricanes" http//www.ready.gov./hurricanes

Cross, Wilbur. Gullah Culture in America. Winston-Salem, North

Carolina, John F. Blair, trade paperback edition, 2012

Fodor's In Focus: Charleston w/Hilton Head and the Low Country, N. Y., N. Y. Random House,2013

Fuller, John, "How Tea Works" W http/Wikipedia.org/ "Tea," Whttp: //en.wikipedia, org/ wiki/tea

Gascoyne, Keven Francis Marchand, Jasmin Desharnais and Hugo Americi. Tea: History, Terroirs, Varieties, Ont, Richmond Hills, Firefly Books, 2011.

Kew: Royal Botanical Gardens: "Camellia Sinensis (tea)" information compiled by Michiel van Slageren, Mark Nesbitt, Tony Hall, Emma Tredwell and Helen Sanderson, September 11, 2025 Kew Royal Botanic Gardens, Kew Royal Botanic Gardens, www.kew.org/ science-conservation/plants—fungi/ camelia-sinensis tea

Official Site: "Gullah Geechee: Cultural Heritage Corridor" Clyburn, James E. http://gullahgeecheecorridor. Org/?itemid+102

Pethonkoukis, James, reviewer. Grant, James. *The Forgotten Depression 1921: The Crash That Cured Itself*, N.Y. Times Book Review, 1/23/15

Raymond, Jackson. "Charleston's African-American Heritage," http://www.africanamericacharlston.com/ Gullah.htmt

The Holy Bible, Revised Standard Version. Translated from the original tongues, being the version set forth A.D. 1611, Revised A.D. 1881-1885 and A.D. 1901, compared with the most ancient authorities and revised A. D. 1946-1952, copyright, 1962 by the World Publishing Company, Old Testament Song of Solomon 8:6, New Testament John 11-21

Wikipedia, "Henry Scott Holland", http//www.wikipedia. org/"Henry Scott Holland"

Wikipedia. "Wallace Hume Carothers" http//www. Wikipedia.org/ "Wallace Hume Carothers"

Wikipedia, Molloy, James Lynam, "Love's Old Sweet Song,"
  http//en.wikipedia.org/Love % 27s_Old-Sweet-Song
Many thanks to Gail Roncevic for her excellent editing!